Once Upon a Beach

Diane M. Pratt

Published by Diane M. Pratt, 2023.

This is a work of fiction. Similarities to real people, places, or events are entirely coincidental.

ONCE UPON A BEACH

First edition. August 11, 2023.

ISBN: 979-8223057659

Written by Diane M. Pratt.

Table of Contents

Chapter 1

Poppy Hartman eased the Jeep to a stop in the narrow, paved driveway and gazed at the beach cottage she'd just bought an hour ago. It was small, it was adorable, almost thirty years old, and it needed some work, but once she'd replaced the cedar shingles, patched a few holes then repainted every wall, did something with the kitchen, and replaced the flooring, it would be as close to perfect as she wanted it to be. If only there wasn't *soooo* much work to be done.

But really, it was better this way. She hadn't wanted a new house that was perfect for someone else. She'd wanted a beach cottage and for what she'd been able to afford, 333 Surf Drive in Belvedere, Massachusetts was the winner, all because of its cosmetic challenges.

Taking her new house keys in hand and following the short walk to her new front door, she stepped into the living room and looked around at the empty rooms, again seeing the potential, as she had when she'd first viewed the cottage. Yes, her little house needed work, but she had two weeks of vacation time to make a serious dent in her things-to-do list and really start to make it her own. She wished she could have had the floors redone before she moved in, but she'd make it all work somehow. Maybe she'd replace the carpet with wood flooring. Or maybe tile that looked like wood.

Like everything else, the kitchen was original to the cottage and just as dated, and Poppy had resigned herself to another hard fact; there would be no gutting, no new cabinets, and no new sink. For now, she would make do with painting the cabinets and replacing the hardware and the faucet. The stove and refrigerator were still functioning, and she hoped they'd continue to function until she had the money to replace them. She thought of the kitchen she'd had for the past three years, with its gleaming granite counter tops, stainless steel appliances, and the island with counter seating. But the past had no place in her present and thinking about it served no purpose.

Stepping out onto her roomy deck, which ran the width of her cottage and provided enough space for a few chairs and a small table, she looked beyond to the real treasure, the beautiful Atlantic Ocean. When she took the steps off the deck and walked the two hundred feet down the sandy incline of her private beach, she'd be at the water's edge.

There wasn't a single tree to be seen on her side of the street as far as she'd been able to see, but there were a few scrub pines in the yards on the other side of Surf Drive. She was fine with having no trees. All the better to see the pink and white beach roses that bloomed all around her foundation. As she'd noticed before, the air was salty and fresh and divine and she pictured herself sitting out on her deck every night to watch the sun setting. It would be wonderful.

Her nearest neighbors' cottages were closer than she would have liked, maybe only about a hundred feet away, and her cottage wasn't all that far from the street, but on a more positive note, her sandy yard would never need mowing, or any kind of maintenance.

Poppy thought about how meticulous Connor had always been about their lawn, watering and mowing and fertilizing so often she'd wondered if he would ever be really happy with the way it looked.

For the most part, as more time had passed, she'd been able to stop thinking of the three years she'd been with Connor in their beautiful new home as wasted time. But, hell's bells, she was already thirty-five, and ...

Don't think about it, or him, or anything else that serves no purpose.

She took a breath and reminded herself the check she'd received when they'd sold the house and gone their separate ways had made it possible for her to buy her very own beach cottage. That was what she needed to focus on.

Heading back to the Jeep to unload boxes with the few things she'd decided to keep, she carried them to the kitchen and pushed them against the half wall that separated the room from the living room. Maybe she'd take that little wall out to make the space feel a little bigger, more of an open concept, only on a much smaller scale. And maybe if she had a clue how to knock down walls she'd think about trying it. But since she didn't have a clue, it was probably wiser to just paint it and use the little shelf on top to display something. Maybe even a houseplant she might be able to keep alive.

When her phone chirped with a text, she was relieved to see her furniture delivery would be arriving in about an hour. She could use that hour to either haul in the clothes that were taking up all the seats in the Jeep, then maybe change into her cutoffs and a tee shirt, or she could get to the store to buy a broom, dust pan, and waste basket, which seemed to be the most pressing items at the moment. There was just so much she needed to get...

Locking up, she hurried to her Jeep, fingers crossed that the summer traffic wouldn't delay her return and make her late.

HAMILTON WHEELER STOOD at a living room window and watched as the brunette in the cottage next door ferried a couple of boxes inside before returning to her Jeep to reverse out of the drive, then he focused on what his brother had just said. "Linc, I don't have time to gut the place. I'm just going to make it look better than it does."

"You have a couple of weeks. Can't you knock down that wall?" Lincoln Wheeler pointed. "And what's so interesting out the window?"

"Maybe if I were a pro I could do it, but we both know I'm not. I'll make your place look better, but that's all I can promise. If you wanted a showplace, you should have bought a showplace."

"I can't afford a showplace, Ham."

"Or a pro. So you're stuck with your brother. Luckily for you, I work for free."

"Yeah. And I've still got school loans to pay off," Linc said.

"Welcome to adulthood, kid."

"Thanks, ancient one. And thanks for letting me stay in your house. I don't think my boss would appreciate Cottage Reno 101 in the background of my virtual meetings."

"Not as if I have much choice since your place has only one bedroom and a poor excuse for a couch." Ham gestured to the outdoors. "You've got a new neighbor."

Linc walked to the window to take a look. "Where?"

"She just went out. Drives a red Jeep."

"What's she look like?"

"Female. I'll get started today, now that I know what needs to be done. Just need to grab some tools."

"Thanks, Ham. I really appreciate your help on this," Linc said.

"You're welcome. You did well, Linc. Not many twenty-five-year-olds can say they own a cottage on the beach."

"Even if the cottage is falling apart?"

"It's not that bad." Ham's eyes scanned the walls and ceiling, hoping there weren't any ugly electrical or plumbing surprises that were going to bite his brother at some point down the road. "I'll be back." Maybe he'd leave the sledge hammer at home so Linc didn't get any more demo ideas.

POPPY EYED THE BIG truck that seemed to fill her rearview mirror, hoping it contained her furniture. Stepping a little harder on the gas, she increased the space between them just in case, soon losing the truck. She made it home and had had time to bring in her new purchases before she heard knocking, and she looked through the screen door to see the truck had arrived.

"Homestyle Furniture. Are you Penelope Hartman?" the man on the porch said.

"I am." Poppy pushed open her screen door, then got out of the way of the two men, doing her part by directing them, and in minutes, she was in possession of a bedroom set, couch, end tables, lamps, and a kitchen table and four chairs.

When she was alone again, she walked around and touched all her new furniture, then dropped onto the couch, happy to be able to sit for a minute while she studied her things-to-buy list. It was an impressive two pages long and she didn't want to think what it would all cost.

Break over, she grabbed her purse and headed out to spend a ridiculous amount of money on everything from silverware to bedding. Oh, boy.

Chapter 2

"I'm working on the outside today, since the weather is cooperating," Ham said when he arrived at Linc's cottage on Saturday morning, and his brother's expression made his opinion clear.

"Can't you work in here on the painting? I see the inside more than the outside," Linc said.

"You want to work out there and I'll be in here?" Ham knew Linc wouldn't go for that, and he also knew where he would be working, with or without his brother's blessing. "Those shingles need to be replaced, and I've only got so many days to finish everything. It could rain the next thirteen days and then where would you be?"

"Then go ahead and work outside. I'll go to Home Zone and get the paint."

Ham knew his brother needed to get homeownership figured out the way everyone else had to and he probably should just butt out, but he couldn't see himself standing by and letting Linc make avoidable rookie mistakes. "First you'll need spackle for the dings in the walls, plus the tools to apply it and finish it up. That'll be a putty knife, sandpaper, sponge, and a small bucket."

"So I'll buy all that stuff with the paint. You said the ceilings need to be painted, too?"

Ham looked up at the discoloration caused by decades of neglect. But at least the roof was in decent shape and hadn't sprung any leaks that resulted in water stains. "That's right. I brought rollers and roller sleeves and a couple brushes for the paint. And drop cloths." He eyed the floor. "What are you doing about these floors?"

"Whatever you think works best. I'll see you in a few hours, Ham, once I buy half the hardware store."

Watching his brother leave out the front door, Ham shook his head, then guessed he was no different ten years ago than Linc was now and he should cut his brother some slack. The kid wanted his place to look new, and Ham understood that, but he also understood Linc had no idea how much sweat equity and money it was all going to take. He'd find out the way they all found out. Heading out to the truck, he grabbed the first bundle of cedar shingles and his pry bar and brought them to the left side of the cottage.

AS POPPY AWAITED HER parents' arrival on Saturday so she could give them a tour of the inside of her cottage, then feed them lunch as a thank you for the advice she hoped to receive, she had a feeling she'd be feeding them quite a few times this summer to show her appreciation. Hearing unidentified sounds outside, she had to check three different windows before she located the source, a dark-haired bearded man in jeans and a white tee shirt working on the cottage next door. Watching him pry off a few shingles and hearing the pieces of wood crack as he worked, she pictured herself doing the same thing on her own cottage and she groaned. He clearly knew what he was doing, but what was also clear was the fact it would be hard, strenuous work, and she was dreading it. Not to mention removing the old shingles was only half the job. Then she'd have to figure out how to nail the new shingles up in straight lines and trim them so they'd fit around the windows and the doors and the roof line. Maybe she should have taken a carpentry class in college.

Hearing a car outside, she went to her screen door to see the cavalry had arrived, and both her parents were smiling as they walked to meet her. "Hi, Mom and Dad. Welcome to my little cottage." Poppy gave them each a hug, so relieved to see them, then she stood back, hands clasped. "Want to start with the outside?"

"Yes, let's. Poppy, this is about the cutest house I've ever seen," Lauren Hartman said. "You must love it so much already."

"I do, and I'll love it even more once the work is finished."

"Are you having new siding put on? More cedar shingles like these?" Nick Hartman asked, rapping his knuckles on the outside wall.

"Yes. Do you think I can do it myself? How hard do you think it will be?"

Nick gestured to the cottage next door. "I think that's how hard it will be. Maybe you can ask that guy for an estimate to do yours, too."

Poppy glanced at the bearded man's back, then looked at her father. "You don't think I can do it, Dad?"

"Maybe you can pick your battles, honey," Lauren said.

"I know you're both probably right, but I really wish I didn't have to pay someone else to do it." Watching the man next door, who was in the process of breaking off another shingle, she decided to get it over with. "I'll be right back."

Ham heard footsteps approaching, knowing it wasn't Linc, and he muttered his opinion of interruptions. He wasn't in the mood for socializing and he hoped whoever it was didn't plan to stay long.

"Excuse me," Poppy said, standing out of the man's reach in case he started swinging that scary looking bar around again. When he finally turned to look at her she took a step back, unprepared for the sight of the bluest eyes she'd ever seen. It hadn't occurred to her until that moment this could very well be her neighbor, and not someone hired to do the shingling. "Um. Hello. Do you live here?"

"No." Maybe she'd leave him in peace now.

That answered that question. "Then would you be able to give me a quote to shingle my cottage? After you remove the old shingles, too, I mean. I need the whole job done." The man's unblinking stare made her wonder if she needed to repeat herself. There wasn't so much as a hint of a smile or basic friendliness and she wondered what his problem was.

The brunette was beautiful, startlingly so, but Ham reminded himself he'd come across beautiful before, and he knew what was too often lurking right below the surface. "No."

"No? You won't give me a quote?" Poppy wished her parents had walked over with her so they'd be hearing this.

"Correct." Staring at the woman wasn't going to get the job done, and he slid his eyes back to the wall in front of him, hoping she'd take the hint and leave him alone. The last thing he needed was having a woman like her in his face.

Incredible. Poppy had been exposed to rudeness in her time. Of course she had. Everyone had. But being treated to such a heavy dose of it by someone who was in the home-improvement business was an entirely new and unexpected experience. "Please forgive my intrusion on your unspeakably busy day. Had I known you were retiring after you finished working on this cottage, I never would have troubled you with such a Herculean task. And may I say you look somewhat well preserved for a man of what, sixty, or is it sixty-five?"

Chapter 3

Ham gritted his teeth but kept his eyes on the job at hand, appreciating the fact he was now guaranteed to be left alone by the woman. Just the way he wanted it. Jamming the pry bar where it needed to be, he broke off the next piece of cedar shingle. Then the next. And he'd continue to break them off until he finished this side of the cottage, then he'd nail up the new shingles and move on to the next side.

Wow. He had to be the rudest man in the entire town of Belvedere, including the influx of tourists who arrived in droves every year when summer began, and Poppy knew if she were smart she would forget about him and his shingles and his tools and his horrible attitude. Heading across the sand toward her parents, who were checking out her beach, Poppy pasted on a smile.

"What does he charge?" Nick asked.

"He's too high," Poppy said. "I'll try someone else. Who's ready to see the inside? I promise you'll be amazed."

"It's always a good idea to get a few quotes," Lauren said. "And we can't wait to see the inside of your cottage."

"First let's step onto the deck and gaze at the amazing view. Dad, you'll notice there's no grass, which means no yardwork. Mom, the roses are lovely but they're loaded with thorns, so make sure you don't get too close. And inside these French doors you'll find all kinds of opportunity for improvement. So keep an open mind." Poppy held the door and kept her eyes on her parents' faces as they stepped inside. Before she followed, she couldn't help sending one more glance at the barbarian next door.

And that *beard*; it wasn't the typical stubble beard that ninety-nine percent of men chose to grow, it was a full on, serious, mountain man beard. Who even wore a beard like that, especially in the summer?

But never mind him. He didn't live next door to her, she wouldn't have to look at him once he finished working on that cottage, and she would find a reasonable human being, one with at least basic social graces, to replace her shingles.

Barbarian.

WELL PRESERVED FOR a man of sixty, was he? Ham shoved the pry bar into the crevice with more force than was necessary, splintering the cedar and making his job more difficult than it needed to be. Maybe he should have told Linc to rent a dumpster so he could toss the broken pieces inside instead of trying to cram them all into the trash barrel, which was barely adequate and would mean repeated trips to the dump.

Glancing toward the house next door to see the yard was empty but may not remain empty, he decided taking a few breaks during the day wasn't a bad idea. Maybe he'd make the first dump run once Linc returned and got set up inside doing whatever he'd decided to start on first.

His brother was going to hate painting the ceilings. Hell, Linc would probably hate doing all of it, but he needed to learn basic skills, and Ham was happy to teach him. If he knew his brother, he'd drag his feet this weekend, knowing Ham would be there to pick up wherever Linc left off. Ham eyed the next shingle and hoped lunch would be happening soon.

"I KNOW YOU'RE GOING out for dinner tonight, so I made sandwiches for lunch. Is that all right?" Poppy said, pulling the covered platter from the fridge.

"Sandwiches are great," Lauren said. "Poppy, your cottage is just beautiful. I love the way you've already set up everything. Your bedroom is gorgeous, the living room looks so nice, and this kitchen set is perfect."

"Thanks, Mom. I appreciate your kind words. It's hard to see beyond the state my cottage is in, but I'll see it once I fix up the walls and paint everything in sight."

"What color paint do you want to use?" Lauren asked.

"I'm not sure yet. I want it to really have a beachy feel to it. Maybe blue and green or yellow? I'll see."

"Your denim couch is definitely beachy," Lauren said. "It's so pretty and comfortable."

"I can give you a hand with the painting or anything else you want to do," Nick said. "Just not the shingles. You want a pro handling that."

"I can paint, too," Lauren said.

"I appreciate your offer, Mom and Dad. I'll see what I can get done myself, and I'll let you know when I hit some trouble. Now let's have some lunch."

"NICE JOB PACKING ALL that in your trunk," Ham said, standing beside Linc in the driveway as they surveyed the open lid of Linc's Camry.

"Thanks. I can't wait to trade in this poor excuse for a car and get something new," Linc said. "Maybe a Lexus."

Ham kept his thoughts to himself. If Linc went to price a Lexus he'd be hit with a few hard facts about his paychecks only stretching so far. Maybe he'd decide their parents' hand-me-down Camry wasn't such a bad mode of transportation after all. "Decide where you want to store all this, either in the house or in that little shed, then you can put on some old clothes and get started on painting the ceilings. They should be done before the walls. Just my opinion."

"I'm hungry. Are you hungry?" Linc said. "Maybe I should go pick up something for us to eat."

Ham looked beyond Linc's cottage to the ocean.

And so it begins.

Chapter 4

"This is so freakin' cool."

Ham knew Linc wasn't talking about the roast beef sub in his hand since his brother was staring at the water. "You did well buying this, Linc."

"Thanks to you, Ham, but I'll pay you back. And I know the place needs some work, but it's already in pretty good shape. I guess I'll do what you said and start painting the ceilings after we eat. Unless you want me to help you with the shingles."

"You do the ceilings. We don't want to be bumping into each other out here and I only have one pry bar."

"That works."

Ham glanced next door but the woman hadn't come back outside, which meant she wouldn't be distracting Linc and delaying the ceiling work. "I'll get back to the shingles. When you're ready to start, give me a holler."

"I'm ready now. On a scale of one to ten, how much am I going to hate this job?"

"Give it about a five."

"I can do a five," Linc said.

"Going to have to if you want to get this house into shape." Ham grinned and followed his brother inside.

POPPY WAVED OFF HER parents from the driveway, then she returned to her front door, sparing only a glance at the barbarian, who was still ripping shingles off the side of the house. She looked at the truck in the driveway for some kind of identification, but there were no decals or any name on it, which she thought was odd. But then, so was the man. Maybe he only worked through referrals.

She'd wasted enough time thinking about him and she had better things to do, such as determine what color to paint her rooms. All the same color, or maybe some variety? An accent wall with a different color, or maybe peel and stick wallpaper? Her kitchen and living room should probably be the same color. And the cabinets should definitely be white, to brighten up the small space. The dark gray color they were sporting now just wasn't doing it for her.

The first step was to get to the hardware store for a generous collection of paint samples. And she'd pick up some ceiling paint and painting tools and drop cloths to protect her new furniture. It would have been great if she could have done all the painting before the furniture arrived, but she didn't want to stay either at her parents' house or at a hotel while she got her cottage into perfect shape because she couldn't wait to move in.

Heading out to her Jeep again, she eyed the houses across the street. They were larger than the cottages on her side of Surf Drive, with bigger yards, actual yards covered with lush green grass. Not only could she not afford any of them, but they weren't actually on the beach. Nor were they cottages. She loved her little cottage, and was going to love it even more in no time.

When she returned home, the back of her Jeep filled with painting supplies, she noticed the barbarian was nowhere in sight and the pickup truck that had been parked next door was gone, leaving a silver Camry. The newly replaced shingles looked really nice, and she wondered if the shingling was finished for the day. There was still plenty of daylight left, but maybe the barbarian didn't work all day on Saturdays. Opening the back of her Jeep, she pulled out two of the gallons of ceiling paint and headed for her front door.

"Hello."

She heard the voice and looked around, seeing a man approaching. He looked young, maybe mid-twenties, and he wore a bright smile. "Hello." When he reached her, he extended a hand.

"I'm Linc from next door. Can I help you with those cans?"

"I'm Poppy." She noticed Linc was sporting white paint stains on his hands and his black shorts and knew he was probably busy doing what she'd be busy doing soon. "Thanks, but I've got them."

"I'm happy to hold one so you can open your door," Linc said.

"Thank you, Linc." She nodded to the can she handed to him. "As you can see, my ceilings need to be painted."

"I've been working on mine, but I needed to get outside for a break."

Poppy unlocked her front door and reached for the can of paint. "Thanks for your help."

"You're just moving in?"

"Yesterday."

"My place needs a lot of work, but living on the beach like this? It's all worth the extra work."

"It is," Poppy said.

"Well, you take care. Good luck with your painting."

"Thanks. You, too." She watched Linc for a few moments as he crossed to his own yard, thinking he was about a thousand percent nicer than the barbarian. Returning to the Jeep for the rest of the supplies, she compared the bright, new shingles next door to her old, worn out shingles. She really needed to find someone to take care of hers. Soon.

HAM LIFTED THE EMPTY barrel out of the truck bed and brought it to the back of the cottage then he headed inside to check on Linc's progress.

Remember, you're not his boss.

Finding his brother in the living room, the ceiling looking a damn sight better than it had, Ham was impressed. "Looking good, Linc. You're almost done."

Linc lowered the roller. "I met one of the neighbors, Poppy. She's a babe."

"Which house?" When his brother gestured to the woman's cottage, Ham thought of a few comments he could make, none of which Linc would want to hear. He'd let Linc find out for himself. It would be another good life lesson.

"She's painting her ceilings, too. Maybe I should ask if she needs help."

Maybe you shouldn't. "I'll get going on the back of the house."

"You think I should?" Linc asked.

"I think you should get your place in order before you start on someone else's." That was all Linc needed, to get caught up with a woman Ham suspected was closer to his age than his brother's.

"You're probably right."

I know I'm right. Ham went out onto the deck and eyed the worn out shingles, ready for round two.

Chapter 5

After dinner, Poppy carried a drink out onto her deck, wishing she'd picked up some patio furniture today, but it was only day one, and she could enjoy the evening just as well if she sat on the steps. The hammering from the cottage next door had stopped and she didn't see the barbarian or Linc outside. They could have been on the far side of the cottage, and if she'd felt like it, she could have walked to the water's edge, then turned and gotten a good look at how much of the shingling had been finished. The black pickup truck was back in the driveway, even this late in the day, which she found astonishing since she'd thought tradesmen stopped working at 3:30.

Closing her eyes and just appreciating the sea breeze, the salty smell, and the sun on her face, she mentally planned her Sunday; a whole lot of painting and, with luck, at least one freshened up room. She'd made the difficult decision about which paint colors would be on her walls, but she had to get the ceilings finished first. Opening her eyes, she watched as the waves rolled in to the shore, over and over and over.

"YOU HAVE TIME FOR A beer before you leave?" Linc asked.

Ham was tired after finishing half the cottage, but he could wait a while before he headed home. "Sure."

Linc pulled a couple of bottles from the fridge. "Let's take them outside."

Heading out and settling into the white plastic Adirondack chair, Ham took a drink, his eyes on the waves. "You can watch the sun set from your deck."

Linc leaned closer to his brother's chair. "Or I can watch Poppy." He gestured with his head.

Ham looked toward the woman's cottage, seeing her on her deck steps.

"Think I'll go ask her if she wants to come over for a beer." Linc stood.

That was the worst idea Ham had heard all day. He thought about getting the hell out of there, then thought better of it. Linc hadn't had a lot of experience with women as far as he knew, and Ham could see the writing on the wall. "You sure you want to do that?"

"Why not?"

"Getting too friendly with the neighbors isn't a good idea." Ham took another drink of the Sam Adams, fighting the urge to look at the woman again.

"It's just a beer, Ham."

He sighed as he watched his brother, beer in hand, cross from his deck to the woman's, then he kept his eyes on the woman.

"Hi, Poppy," Linc said.

Poppy hadn't heard anyone approaching on the sand, and was startled to see her neighbor in front of her. Lesson learned. "Hello, Linc."

"Want to come over for a beer?"

That was the last thing she wanted, but she wasn't going to be rude. "Thanks for the invitation, but I've finished my ten-minute break and I have to go in and get back to work."

"Sure," Linc said, nodding. "Maybe another time."

Letting a smile be her answer, Poppy stood and glanced at Linc's deck. There was the barbarian, beer in hand, watching her, and she was so thankful she'd declined. "You have a great night, Linc."

"Thanks, Poppy. You, too."

Ham watched the scenario play out, then kept his eyes on his brother's face after the woman had disappeared inside. Linc didn't look broken up about being refused.

Dropping onto a chair, Linc said, "She's got work to do. Probably more painting."

Maybe she was as asocial as Ham thought.

Maybe Linc had flirted with her and she wasn't interested.

Or maybe Ham being there was the reason she'd said no. It had been clear she hadn't been any more impressed with him than he'd been with her. In the long run, he knew that was best for Linc, if his brother had plans to be over there helping her with her own improvements instead of working on his own. Standing, he said, "I'll be over in the morning to see if I can finish the other side."

"Thanks, Ham. I really appreciate your help."

"Nice work on the living room ceiling. You've got hidden painting talent."

Linc laughed. "Sure I do. See you tomorrow."

"I'll hit the dump first with that load of shingles, then come over."

POPPY HEARD A CAR DOOR slam and stepped to her screen door to see the black pickup leaving. Was that how things worked? Once whoever she found to do her shingles finished for the day, she was supposed to sit on the deck and have a beer with him? Well, if it was, he was going to be one disappointed man.

Turning on her tunes, hearing Whitesnake's "Here I Go Again", she nodded her head to the beat, draped the drop cloths around the kitchen, then lowered the roller sleeve into the paint tray. She was determined to finish at least this small ceiling before she quit for the night. Then tomorrow she'd finish the rest of the ceilings so she could start on the much more interesting wall painting.

She wasn't going to ask her parents for help unless she was desperate and she didn't really see that happening since she had two weeks to finish what she wanted to accomplish. If she couldn't get it all done, then she wasn't the person she thought she was.

It was going to be an exciting couple of weeks, and in the end, she'd have almost a brand new home. Eying the gray cabinets as she slid the roller along, she knew they would give her some trouble because of the sheer number of sides she'd need to paint, but she'd manage and they'd be gorgeous.

Chapter 6

Poppy put down the roller stick and stretched her back. It had taken her most of Sunday, but all her ceilings were painted a crisp and clean white, and as much as she'd like to, she knew she couldn't stand around and admire her handiwork because she was in dire need of another shower.

Or, she thought, walking over to look out the back door at the Atlantic Ocean, she could take a swim, then take a shower. She could see plenty of people out there enjoying themselves, and why shouldn't she? Swimming when she felt like it was one of the reasons she'd wanted her beach cottage, and she needed to make a point of jumping in every chance she got this summer.

In addition to the ever-present sound of cars passing by, a drawback to having a cottage so close to the street, she'd been hearing hammering all day and she wondered who else was doing home improvements on this gorgeous, sunny day.

Pulling on her tankini, she remembered Connor's many comments about it as he tried to convince her she should wear a bikini. After the four years they'd been together, how had he not caught on that she wasn't the bikini type? But then, she hadn't caught on that he didn't want kids, either. Probably because he'd told her he did want them, but she should have realized the truth from other comments he'd made about kids over the years.

Never mind.

Think about right now, and the fact you need a towel before you can go outside. Since she was only taking a quick swim, she'd skip the cover up, and she went out her back door, chin up, ready to enjoy herself at her private beach.

HAM PAUSED WHEN HE saw movement behind the cottage next door, and he turned his head to see the woman. Today she was in a blue swim suit, headed for the water, and she dropped a towel in the sand without pausing. He let his eyes travel from her bare feet to her long hair, then back down.

Yes, she was beautiful. Her face and her body.

Veronica had been beautiful, too. But only on the outside. It was his own damn fault for not realizing that sooner. It had been a year since the breakup, and no woman since had even come close to capturing his interest, a fact he appreciated every damn day.

As he watched the woman dive under the waves, then resurface seconds later, he was thankful she wasn't capturing his interest either, with her dark hair, curvy figure, long legs, and that face. She'd basically called him an old man, and Ham knew that was a good thing.

What wasn't good was the interest Linc seemed to be taking in her. Linc was too young for her in every way, and Ham hoped he didn't have to spell that out for his brother. She could chew Linc up and spit him out before he even realized what was happening, and he didn't want his brother hurt by a woman like that.

When it occurred to him he'd spent minutes staring at her, he knew he needed to get back to work, and he turned his head and refocused on the wall in front of his face. With luck he'd finish the shingles by Monday so he could get inside where there'd be fewer distractions.

"Hey, Ham, you feel like a swim?"

Ham hadn't even heard Linc approach, but now his brother was right beside him, Linc's eyes aimed where his own had been aimed only a minute before. "Maybe once I finish. How's the painting going?"

Linc walked around Ham and stood unmoving as he stared. "I need a break, and I'm going in."

"In the house?"

"In the water. Poppy's swimming, and I want to say hello."

Don't do it, Linc. "Do whatever you think is best. I'm staying right here."

"Ten minutes. That's all I'll be in there," Linc said, heading for the back door.

Ham sent another glance toward the woman, who was now stretched out on her back, floating on the waves, and he hoped she'd be out of the water and back in her house before Linc was outside. The water looked tempting and the thought of swimming, even for a few minutes, was almost irresistible, but he knew he'd have more opportunities to swim in the next two weeks, when he'd be alone. When he went home tonight he'd grab his board shorts and a towel. Just in case.

POPPY WAS IMPRESSED that the barbarian even worked on Sundays, and as she played in the water she eyed the back and side walls of Linc's cottage with their brandsy-new golden shingles. They looked so much nicer than her dried out, curled, split shingles. It was really a shame the barbarian wouldn't even give her a quote, but she hoped she'd be able to find someone the next day who could at least let her know how much and how soon the job could be done.

She saw Linc come out his back door in red and white board shorts, dropping a towel on the railing of his deck before walking toward the water. And possibly her. At least his eyes seemed to be on her, but maybe she was imagining things. Then he raised a hand in a wave, and she heard him say her name, so she waved.

Definitely headed her way, striding into the waves before taking a dive and appearing only a few feet away from her. His smile made him look so young, and she wondered just how young he was.

"Hello, Linc."

"Hi, Poppy."

"Your new shingles look really nice." She watched Linc maneuver himself so he was floating beside her, then he looked back at his cottage.

"Much better than they did," he said.

"I need to find someone to do mine. I finished my ceilings and I'm going to start on the walls."

"Mine are taking a long time, but they're coming along."

Maybe it was Linc's age, or maybe it was his easy going personality, but Poppy felt a little more relaxed each time she spoke with him and so far he was shaping up to be a good neighbor. "How are your floors? I need to replace mine, and I'm looking at the different options."

"Mine have to be replaced, too. I'll probably go with wood."

"I might do tile that looks like planks," Poppy said. "It will be easy to sweep up all the sand I'm probably going to be tracking inside."

"Can you do the tiling yourself?"

"In my dreams I can."

Laughing, he said, "I hear you. In my dreams my place is three stories high with a rooftop deck, and I drive a Lambo."

Ham watched Linc with the woman, telling himself his brother was twenty-five, not seventeen, and he could take care of himself.

But he didn't like what he was seeing.

He didn't like it one damn bit.

Chapter 7

"Any chance you'll let me take a look inside your place?" Linc asked.

Poppy eyed Linc for a few moments as they floated on the gentle waves. "You want to compare the two cottages?"

"Yeah. See which one of us has the most work to do. I'll return the favor if you want. I'm curious."

"You know they had the same owner and they were used as rentals?"

"Which explains a lot," Linc said.

"Such as the kitchen?"

"Exactly."

She was curious as well, and this was a golden opportunity. "I like that idea. Yes. But we should see them soon, before we make many updates."

"How about tonight, after we finish swimming?"

She thought about them possibly tracking sand into hers and knew it wouldn't matter much. "Sounds good." She looked at Linc's cottage, still hearing the endless hammering. "Your shingler certainly has a strong work ethic." Even if he was lacking a personality.

Linc grinned. "He's the best."

Maybe the barbarian was the best shingler on the planet, but good luck to Linc in having to deal with him. "I'm going in now, so any time you're ready to see my cottage in its natural state, you can come over."

"I'll come in, too. I have to get back to the ceilings or I'll be hearing it from Ham."

Ham? She wasn't going to ask who Ham was, and she started swimming for the shore, seeing Linc in her peripheral vision as he swam beside her.

Linc walked with Poppy until she reached her towel, then he said, "How's five minutes sound?"

"That works." Poppy wrapped herself in the towel and headed for her deck as Linc headed for his own cottage. Drying off before she stepped into her kitchen, she stepped inside and went to her room to change.

Ham was finishing the last few shingles on the side wall when Linc appeared, a towel around his neck. "How's the water?"

"Feels great. I'm going over to Poppy's." Knocking on the cottage wall, he said, "This looks awesome, Ham."

"You're going to Poppy's? Why?"

"We're comparing our places to see who has the most work to do. See you in a few."

Ham watched his brother disappear around the back of the cottage, wondering if he should have said something to discourage Linc. Too late now. Picking up the packet of shingles, he headed around the corner to start on the front of the cottage, telling himself to think about shingles, not about what his brother was doing.

His plan fell apart after about ten seconds, but the irritation surging through him made it easier to pound in the nails. Which was a plus, since it meant he'd be finished sooner.

Poppy had changed into shorts and a blue tee shirt by the time she heard knocking at her front door, and she appreciated the fact Linc had not gone to her back door. Clearly the boy had good manners. But maybe she shouldn't think of him as a boy, since boys were rarely able to buy their own homes. Reaching her screen door, she saw he had pulled on a white tee shirt over his board shorts. "Come in, Linc." She watched as he wiped his boat shoes on her porch mat before stepping inside, more evidence of his manners, then his eyes were traveling around her living room and kitchen.

"Ceilings look great," he said.

"Thank you. It's all downhill from there."

"Literally." Linc grinned. "New paint and floors will transform the rooms." He stepped into the kitchen. "What are your plans for this room? I'm thinking about new cabinets and counters for mine."

"I wish I could afford an upgrade, but I'm just going to paint the cabinets white and maybe get a granite counter if I can find a deal. And new flooring. New flooring everywhere, really."

Linc nodded. "It'll look great when you're finished. Your furniture is pretty nice."

"Thanks. It would have been perfect to do all the updating before I had the furniture delivered, but it didn't work out that way."

"Yeah. I wanted to be in my place as soon as I signed the papers, too."

"Is the layout the same as yours?"

"Identical. Can I see the bedroom and bathroom? It's good they left the washer and dryer in the bathroom, right? I had enough of laundromats in college."

Poppy smiled at the look on Linc's face. "It is good. We didn't need that added expense on top of everything else." She followed him, staying in the short hallway while he looked around, nodding.

"I'll show you my place now," he said.

She followed him down the steps and he waited until she was beside him to continue. Looking over at his house, she saw the barbarian was working on the front of the cottage now, but his eyes were on Linc and her as they approached Linc's front door.

"Ham, this is Poppy. Poppy, this is Ham."

This was Ham? She didn't bother saying they'd met, and she would have liked to return the sharp nod he gave her, but she had better manners than that. "Hello."

Ham watched his brother open the door for the woman, Poppy, then follow her inside, and he picked up another shingle, eyes on his hands as he got back to work, wondering what exactly was happening inside.

"They really are identical, aren't they?" Poppy asked, gazing around. "Your ceilings look nice and bright with their new coat of paint."

"As you can see, my furniture needs an upgrade, but I'll see what's happening with the budget after I finish fixing everything up."

"We'll do the best we can with what we have, right?"

"That's right," Linc said. "I'm lucky Ham's willing to help me out so much, or what you see around here is the way it would be staying."

"I'm using vacation time to accomplish as much as I can. I'd love to put in a big picture window to get an even better view of the water, but that's going to have to wait."

"I hear you. Listen, do you think we can exchange numbers? Only because we're neighbors."

Poppy and Connor had done that with all their neighbors, so she didn't consider Linc's request unusual. "Sure." After she'd rattled off her number, Linc gave her his number and she added it to her phone. "What's your last name, Linc?"

"Wheeler. What's yours?"

"Hartman. Thanks for the tour. Good luck with your updating."

"Yeah. You, too, Poppy."

She walked to the front door, Linc behind her, and she wondered if she'd be forced to speak to Ham again. Maybe if she didn't look his way they could both ignore each other. One of them seemed to have already perfected that art. Stepping out onto the front porch, she said, "Bye, now." She heard Linc say goodbye as she walked toward her yard, but didn't hear anything from Ham. *Shocker.*

Ham listened to Linc's summary of the condition of Poppy's cottage and how it compared to his own as he hammered another shingle. When Linc finished his description, Ham waited for what he was afraid would be coming next, but his brother didn't mention that he'd asked Poppy out.

There's a surprise.

Chapter 8

On Monday morning, Poppy heard the hammering again, and she knew exactly who it was. She'd looked earlier and had seen the black pickup again in Linc's driveway, Ham shingling the front of the cottage today, but the Camry had been missing.

Deciding she needed to change her clothing before her trip to Home Zone, she returned to her room to get into something more presentable than her old cutoffs. Pulling on a sundress and slipping into sandals, she grabbed her purse and checked the mirror. Maybe some lipstick would be a good idea.

Stepping outside and locking her front door, she looked at the sky, the now cloud-filled sky, and she was thankful she wasn't working outside. Nor was Ham, apparently, since she could see he'd finished. Linc's cottage looked so great, and she knew she really needed to find someone to do her shingles. Today. Maybe before she allowed herself to start painting any walls. There was motivation for her. She'd return home and make some calls and get something lined up.

HAM HEARD A DOOR SLAM and walked to the front door to see the Jeep next door reversing out of the driveway. Poppy Hartman, according to Linc, who'd announced he now had Poppy Hartman's number. Ham hadn't made any comment, although his thoughts had taken a decidedly downward turn. He was concerned for his brother, but he'd bide his time and if he sensed trouble for Linc, he'd make damn sure to speak up.

Picking up the spackle, he got to work patching the considerable number of dings in the walls. His wandering eyes took in the kitchen cabinets and Formica counter tops, the plastic outlet and switch plate covers, the light fixtures, and the windows. There was so much that could be done to Linc's place, and all it took was money. Tens of thousands of dollars that Linc didn't have yet. But the kid had his head screwed on right, and he would eventually get everything the way he wanted it. Then he'd find a girl and fall in love, then they'd need a bigger place for the kids that would be coming along in a few years. He knew Linc wanted kids, and Ham hoped like hell Linc wouldn't fall in love with a girl who only pretended to want them.

Finishing the spackling took longer than he'd expected, and he added sand paper to his mental list of things to pick up at Home Zone while he was there checking out the flooring options. Grabbing his keys, he headed out.

IT WAS JUST SO EASY for Poppy to lose herself during her trips to Home Zone, between the cabinets and the paint and the appliances and light fixtures and carpeting and doors and windows and everything she wished she had the money to buy.

But at least she could afford the gallons of paint she needed, and she went to the paint counter, paint sample in hand, to wait for her turn to give the woman behind the counter her request. It had been close, between Ocean Air and White Rain, but Poppy was sure she'd made the right choice with Ocean Air. Part of her reasoning was that Connor would have hated it. Maybe she was being petty, or maybe she was just having things her own way instead of having to compromise over every single little thing. She was so done with compromising, and losing.

Strolling the aisles as she waited for the paint to be mixed, she made her way to the tile section. Flooring was going to be a challenge, but she knew Home Zone would install it if she didn't want to do it herself. And she knew there was no way she could do it herself. Every inch of floor space would be covered in the same material, and there was too much room for error. Her cottage needed to be as perfect as she could afford to make it, and she wasn't going to skimp on the floors.

And there it was. Marina. It really looked like wood but she knew it would be a smarter choice. It was very pretty and would transform her cottage, and it would look beautiful with the Ocean Air paint. Things were really coming together and she wished she had someone with her to share her joy.

Looking up from the tile, she met the eyes of Ham, who stood only a few feet away from her, his usual expression continuing to make it clear he was the last person she'd ever be able to share any joy with.

Ham had noticed the brunette from a distance, and since she'd been headed the same direction he'd been going, he'd followed her. Maybe he hadn't dated or been interested in a woman for the past twelve months, but his eyes were still functioning and he was still capable of recognizing an attractive woman without any need of things going anywhere. Then she turned her head and he was hit with a smile that knocked him back a step. Poppy Hartman was not who he was expecting, and he suspected his mouth was hanging open. He had nothing to say to this woman, and he suspected she had nothing to say to him, which was better for all concerned.

Just because the man was a barbarian didn't mean Poppy was. "Hello." Unsurprised when she received only a nod like the one he'd given her the day before, she returned her eyes to the tile before pulling out her phone to take a shot of Marina before leaving the aisle in search of sales help.

Ham watched Poppy Hartman walk away, hips swaying, dress swinging around her bare legs, long hair bouncing, then he reminded himself he wasn't there to enjoy the scenery.

Chapter 9

By the time Poppy left Home Zone with gallons of Ocean Air for the walls and Alabaster for the cabinets, both kitchen and bathroom, she had arranged for someone to come to her cottage to give estimates on the cedar shingles and the tiling jobs. Even if this someone wouldn't be coming until Wednesday, she still had plenty of painting to do to keep her occupied. Hours of painting. Days of painting. And she needed to finish it all before the flooring was put in.

Reaching her driveway, she saw the black pickup truck was again parked at Linc's cottage, the Camry still missing. She was curious about the barbarian. Maybe she should think of him as Ham, a name she'd never come across in her thirty-five years. But having been given the name Penelope, she was no one to comment on unusual names. She was thankful her parents had given her a good nickname and that most people were happy to call her Poppy. It should have occurred to her something wasn't quite right when Connor had always refused to call her anything but Penelope.

After hauling in all the paint cans and setting them up on the linoleum floor in the kitchen, Poppy eyed the cabinets. "You're up first."

An hour later, as "Total Eclipse of the Heart" was wrapping up, she took a step back to assess her progress. "Alabaster, we are killing it. Look at those beauties." The white paint was transforming the kitchen, even before the walls were painted and the flooring was replaced. It was all going to be gorgeous. Starting another hour-long iTunes playlist, she danced around the kitchen to "Don't You Want Me", singing along with The Human League. Today was a *wonderful* day.

HAM TOLD HIMSELF HE'D had enough of a break and he needed to get back inside and return to the kitchen to get started on the walls. The sooner he finished the painting, the sooner he could lay the flooring, and the way the work was progressing, he doubted he'd need to spend the full two weeks working on the cottage.

At Home Zone he'd overheard Poppy Hartman's request for quotes on flooring and shingling, and as he worked he gave a few second's thought to giving her his own quote for the work, providing he'd have the time.

When common sense returned, he shook his head. *You're an amateur*. Not to mention Poppy Hartman is no one he wanted to get mixed up with. No, she wasn't Veronica. No, she wasn't a redhead. But she still had too much of an edge to her, and she hadn't taken well to the word "No".

But if he gave her a price, and she agreed to that price, the work would keep him busy until he had to return to Couril, and the money he'd earn could go toward more improvements for Linc. He heard a woman's voice raised in song, and it took him only a few moments to identify "Don't You Want Me".

Glancing toward Poppy Hartman's cottage, he knew he'd heard much worse and he wondered as he went inside if she ever performed on karaoke nights at Bud's Lounge.

POPPY HAD JUST FINISHED the last kitchen cabinet and was admiring the new look when she heard the knocking. After resting the brush on the can of paint, she headed for the front door. The barbarian was here to see her? No. His name was Ham. "Hello."

"I overheard you at Home Zone, and if you're interested, I can give you quotes for your shingles and your floors."

Before she had a chance to ask the man why he'd done an about-face, Ham had left her as quickly as he'd appeared.

Would it hurt to have something to compare the Home Zone quotes with?

Of course not.

Did she think Ham would be able to beat Home Zone's quotes?

That was more difficult to determine. The facts were Linc was using Ham, and Linc was clearly not in the millionaire tax bracket since he was living next to Poppy, nor did he drive a late model car. In addition, Ham's truck didn't proclaim his profession, which was strange and kind of a gray area. Maybe there was an excellent reason he didn't have signage on that truck. But signage wasn't what mattered right now. She should get those quotes. There was no obligation. And if Ham turned out to be a jerk, she'd just fire him.

She marched out the door and aimed for Linc's cottage.

HAM WAS STIRRING THE Moonshine paint as he eyed the kitchen walls. There wasn't a lot of wall space in the kitchen and he should finish both coats in less than an hour. Hearing knocking, he looked toward the front door and bit back a grin when he saw Poppy Hartman on the porch. Taking the short walk over, he said, "Can I help you?"

Poppy heard "Is This Love" playing, then told herself not to get sidetracked because Ham was listening to Whitesnake. Plenty of people listened to Whitesnake. "I'd like to hear your quotes for the shingles and the floors."

"I'll be over later."

She hoped his quote was going to be more than a dollar figure, since it would be nice to know a breakdown of charges, but if his quoting skills were anything like his so-called conversational skills, she was going to be disappointed. "All right, then." Turning, she stepped off the porch and headed home. He was certainly something else. Unbelievable, really. But she didn't need to accept his quotes. She would go with whoever had the lowest price. That was what everyone did.

Ham watched until Poppy Hartman disappeared into her house before returning to the kitchen, wondering if he'd made a mistake. Maybe it had been more like a huge mistake. But he could quote her so high she'd never go for it if he decided he wouldn't be able to deal with her.

As he dipped the brush into the paint, he reviewed the conversations he'd had with Poppy Hartman.

No. She was nothing like Veronica, either on the outside or the inside.

Chapter 10

As Ham painted, he made mental calculations for the estimates he would give Poppy Hartman. He had the option of getting a quote from Home Zone for the same work at Linc's place since it was identical to the one next door, then lowering the price, but that was not only sneaky, he wouldn't be able to get their quote until after they'd quoted Poppy Hartman. He knew what he'd need in the way of shingles, so it was only the quantity of tiles he had to measure for.

Finishing his second coat on the living room walls, he lay the roller on the paint tray and stepped back, the drop cloth crackling under his feet. The place was looking much better, and it was only Monday.

Grabbing his sandwich from the fridge, he headed for the deck. Despite the cloud cover it was a nice day, and he appreciated being off his feet for a few minutes. Glancing next door as he took a drink, he didn't see any action either on the deck or around the exterior, and he focused his gaze on the water instead, deciding after he finished lunch he'd head over next door before he started working on the bedroom walls.

After crossing the sandy ground between the cottages and stepping onto the small front porch, he heard "Hungry Eyes" playing from inside and he pressed the doorbell, wondering if it would be heard over the music.

Poppy headed into the living room when she heard the bell, her eyes on the wall clock as she lowered the volume on her phone, and she wondered how it had gotten this late. And there was Ham at her door. “Hello.” Pushing the screen door open, she stepped back to give the man room to come in.

“Okay if I look around?” Ham noted a paint stain on her fingertips and another on her bare thigh below the rough edge of her cutoffs. When his eyes landed on her bare feet, he looked away when he saw the pink nail polish. He’d always had a thing about pink polish.

“Yes.” Poppy wondered why he didn’t carry so much as a piece of paper or a pen, at least as far as she could see, but she supposed it went along with his lack of advertising on the pickup truck. Should she follow him around? It wasn’t as if her cottage was huge, and she could probably watch him no matter where he went if she stood in the middle of her living room.

Ham pulled out his tape measure to get some dimensions.

“Do you want me to hold one end?” she asked. Her mother always helped her father when they measured anything in the house.

“Got it.” He added the dimensions to his phone as he went, surprised Poppy Hartman would offer to help. Veronica had never wanted any part of his “puttering around”. Stepping into the kitchen, he reminded himself bringing up the past was not improving his present.

Poppy watched Ham work, marveling that someone who worked with people, with paying *customers*, could be so solitary. It had been her experience that delivery people and trades’ people were social and she’d never had anyone come to her door or inside her home who hadn’t at least said *something*.

Ham hadn't even said a dozen words, and she bit back a smile wondering if he was going to give her a verbal quote or show her the number on his phone. Maybe he'd send her a text. That would actually be best because then she'd have it recorded.

His silence was amazing.

His entire attitude was amazing.

She wondered if it was because he disliked her and she supposed that was possible since she had made that crack about his age. Maybe he hadn't appreciated it in such a big way he'd never think of her as anything more than a rude person he didn't want anything to do with. Which didn't explain why he'd offered to give her quotes for two major jobs.

Ham couldn't help comparing Poppy Hartman's cottage to Linc's. The structures were identical, but the new wall colors and the furniture were quite different. Linc was using second-hand furniture for now, and Poppy Hartman's was all new and of good quality, but he guessed that was easily explained. He'd known as soon as he gazed into her eyes she was closer to his age than Linc's. Life had thrown her some curve balls, but those hadn't diminished her smile, or at least the few smiles he'd seen on her. When she'd been with Linc she'd looked pretty damn happy. As had Linc.

Finished with the measuring, he added the last numbers and returned to the living room where she was waiting, arms crossed in what he considered a defensive pose. Maybe she was afraid of what she thought he was going to tell her. "I'll get you numbers this afternoon." Her arms slid down until her hands slipped into her front pockets.

"Thanks." This barely-there conversation was getting on her nerves. "I want the Marina tile. Are you doing Linc's floors, too? He told me he's going with wood." She didn't care that it was none of her business what Linc did, because no matter how Ham felt about her question, surely he'd have to say *something*.

Wouldn't he?

"Likely." Likely? He knew damn well he'd be doing the flooring.

"Since the cottages are probably the same dimensions, you'd only need to measure one. And you already know what the shingling quote will be since you did Linc's, right? Do you want to give me just a verbal quote on that?"

She'd crossed her arms again, and her eyes looked as though she didn't expect he would give her what she wanted. Smart woman. "I'll get you numbers this afternoon."

The man was incredible. "How about this? I can give you my number and you can text the quote or quotes to me, then you won't even have to talk to me at all since you've made it clear that's a nightmare for you."

He stared into Poppy Hartman's fiery eyes and felt the first stirrings of unease. Any dealings he chose to have with her were not going to end well for him if he wasn't scrupulously careful. "I'll be back in four hours."

She watched him stride to her door and let himself out, carefully closing her screen door so it wouldn't slam. Then his eyes met hers and the fact he caught her glowering at him didn't bother her one damn bit.

Ham crossed the sandy yards and pulled open Linc's screen door.

Fiery and sarcastic could be a dangerous combination in a woman.

Add that combination to a face he might never be able to forget and it only ratcheted up the danger.

Chapter 11

After another trip to Home Zone, Ham had the costs he needed for Linc's and Poppy Hartman's floors. Returning to Linc's driveway, he eyed the cottage next door, knowing he was ready with the quotes, but he'd told her four hours and four hours it would be. It would give him time to finish the painting.

Heading inside, it finally sunk in he was going to have too much time on his hands unless he was able to work on both cottages. Otherwise he'd be wasting his vacation time hanging around. Which meant he might need to adjust the quotes for Poppy Hartman. Make them more attractive to her. Picking up the roller again, he decided the idea required a little more thought.

When Poppy Hartman's face accompanied the thought, he knew he needed to focus on something else. The wall in front of his face was a good start. Or he could think about the Red Sox being in first place for the first time this season. Or he could think about the Patriots' upcoming season, wondering if they'd win their pre-season games. There was a bounty of things he could think about.

No. She was in his head. Putting down the roller, he pulled out his phone to send a text to Lawson. "Bud's tonight?" It was karaoke night, and he and Lawson hadn't been there for weeks, not since the tourist season had started, which meant there would be new faces up on the small stage. It would be about impossible not to think about what was happening in front of him instead of wondering what Poppy Hartman might be doing at that moment.

Unless she showed up at Bud's. He'd only heard her voice once, but she'd sounded pretty good. Better than a lot of what he heard on that stage. And if she did show up, climbing onto that stage to belt out "Don't You Want Me", there was no reason why she shouldn't be in his head, since she'd be in the head of every other guy in the place. He put the roller down and as he left the house, he felt his phone vibrate with the text from Lawson.

No Bud's tonight. Maybe next week.

POPPY WAS ENJOYING a tall glass of ice water as she gazed out the back door at the waves when she heard knocking. Four hours couldn't have passed already. Checking the time, she saw it had only been ninety minutes, but there was Ham at her front door, probably about to say something she wasn't going to like.

As she walked toward him, he brushed a hand down his beard, a move she hadn't seen him make yet, and she wondered what it signified. Maybe she'd find out if she accepted his quotes and saw much more of him. Or maybe she'd never find out. The man was so incredibly silent, and she wasn't used to that. Connor talked all the time, and...

Hell's bells. She needed to stop comparing every man she met to Connor.

Right now she needed to decide if she should speak through the screen or let Ham inside again. When her hand reached out to open the door, she guessed she had her answer. Then he was standing right in front of her and she looked up at him. The man was *tall*. Not gigantic tall, just tall. Maybe half a foot taller than she was in her bare feet and she had never in her life been mistaken for petite.

Would he speak first or would they stare at each other until he walked away without explaining what he'd come over to explain? Maybe he really was a barbarian, although a nice looking barbarian. Quite handsome, really. She didn't typically like the looks of a thick beard, but Ham was pulling it off quite well. It looked really soft, and she wondered what it felt like. Crossing her arms so she wouldn't make the mistake of reaching out to touch it, she heard herself say, "Isn't your beard really hot in the summer?"

"No."

No seemed to be his favorite word. Maybe she'd try a question that wouldn't earn her another one. "I presume you're here to give me quotes for the shingling and flooring, and not because of my witty conversation."

He'd noticed she'd done something to her hair, tying it back, although half of it seemed to have fallen out of whatever was holding the rest of it, and her cheeks were flushed pink, possibly from the warmth of the day, but her question got him refocused pretty damn quick. He gave her one quote, then waited for her reaction. First there were raised eyebrows, then her lips twisted before opening.

"That's for both jobs?"

"Yes."

"With or without the shingles and tiles and whatever supplies you need?"

"With."

She had expected a higher price, and it made her wonder what Home Zone was going to charge. "And when would you be able to start?"

"As soon as I finish with Linc's."

She was going to lose at least two days waiting for Home Zone's quotes, but she knew she had to get those quotes. "May I have the quotes, or quote, in writing? Since I don't know anything about you other than you did a good job on Linc's shingles and you work Saturdays and Sundays. Do you ever get days off?" She shouldn't have asked that of him even if it was something she would have asked any other workman who came to her house. "Once I hear from Home Zone, I'll let you know if I accept your offer."

It wasn't unreasonable of her to ask for it in writing. He'd have done the same. "What's your email address?"

Poppy recited it for him, watching as he added it to his phone, then he walked to her door without a word and was gone again. She wondered what he'd be like after a beer or two. Or maybe a glass of wine. She'd never known anyone who was so damned silent. Did he have a girlfriend? Was she silent, too, or did she talk all the time? Poppy knew she wasn't exactly a Chatty Cathy, but she could form a few sentences when she was with other people. She could even talk to herself. Maybe Ham had lengthy chat sessions with himself when no one was around. Maybe he was over at Linc's house right now talking up a storm.

When her phone pinged with an email, she pulled it from her back pocket to investigate. There was Ham's quote, spelling out supplies, labor, and total. Succinct. Just like his euphemistically called *conversations*. She sent her own response, then returned to her painting.

Ham stared at his phone, wondering what Poppy Hartman would have to say next. She didn't make him wait very long.

"Thank you ever so much for taking so much time from your busy day to type out this highly detailed explanation of how you plan to tile my floors and shingle my cottage. I sincerely apologize for making you wait until either Wednesday or Thursday of this week until I let you know if I will be requiring your services, but I am sure you understand, being the professional you are. Very truly yours, Poppy Hartman"

Slipping the phone into his back pocket, he picked up the roller and dipped it into the pan.

Then he smiled.

Chapter 12

Ham was on Linc's deck on Wednesday morning with a glass of iced tea, watching the waves and the few early beach visitors, when he heard a door slam. Doubting whoever it was would be in Linc's driveway, he stood to take a look around and saw the Home Zone pickup in Poppy Hartman's drive and a man approaching her front door.

He knew his quotes would be lower than the pro's were since he wasn't in it for the money, something he wasn't going to admit to anyone because no one would understand. He barely understood it himself. His dealings with Poppy Hartman so far had been the catalyst, he knew that, and if he were able to work in her proximity for a few days, really see what she was like, the contact would go a long way toward convincing him it might be time to think about the possibility of a woman in his future. He was looking at the whole thing as an experiment, of sorts.

Except the experiment had already begun, even if he hadn't realized it at the time. It started the moment Poppy Hartman first breached Linc's property line and asked about getting a quote for the shingling. Then she'd questioned him about his beard on Monday, but he hadn't gotten a sense of her approval or disapproval.

Veronica had been anti-beard and had made it clear she expected Ham to be clean shaven, which was one of the reasons he'd grown the beard after the breakup. His hair had also been a constant torment for her, and she'd frequently shown him photos of how she wanted him to have it cut. A couple of times, to keep peace in the house, he'd acquiesced, but he hadn't liked the way his hair looked. Now he wore it longer and thicker than he ever had, and there was peace in the house round the clock.

Hearing voices, he came out of his head and looked next door to see Poppy Hartman and the man walking the perimeter of her house. Taking another drink, he watched them through the balusters of the deck, wishing the railing height was a few inches lower, but the pair was moving along and they disappeared around the back of the cottage in what seemed like seconds. There were no chairs, or any kind of furniture, on the other deck, and he wondered if Poppy Hartman had plans to get anything out there.

When Linc had stopped by the night before to check on things, he'd told Ham he'd decided not to get new cabinets yet. Instead he wanted them painted white, "just the way Poppy was doing it". He'd even told him he wanted the same paint color she used, which meant Ham would be making another trip to her cottage for the name.

POPPY ABSORBED THE key parts of Victor's explanation, discarding the interesting but irrelevant portions, and she couldn't help but compare his conversational style with Ham's. Victor was hands-down the conversation king, and she imagined what it would be like if she agreed to Home Zone's quotes, and the workers who came to her cottage were as talkative as Victor. But her decision was going to be all about the money. Because it was always about the money.

After Victor had seen everything he needed to see and measured the rooms, as Ham had, he'd gone to his truck to work up the quote, which he said he'd email to her. She stood in her kitchen, wondering how the quotes would compare, both visually and numerically.

Walking around while she waited, she looked next door and saw Ham on a deck chair. Ham-sightings were rare since the man never seemed to take any breaks. She hadn't seen Linc around for days, and Ham seemed to be there all day every day, and overnight. Linc was either really trusting or, or, well, she didn't know what other options there could be. And she wouldn't ask Ham since all she'd get would be a one word answer. Not to mention it was none of her business.

Checking her email, she saw Victor, AKA Home Zone, had sent his and she opened the attachment. *Wow*. It was more than double what Ham had quoted. Heading to her front door, she saw Victor approaching, and after a quick conversation, he was on his way.

Poppy stared at his quote again and knew what she had to do. The only question was, how soon did she want to do it? Stepping outside, she headed for Linc's deck. She saw the instant Ham noticed her, then she kept her eyes on his until she reached the stairs to the deck. How did she want to put this? The man disliked the use of an excess of words, so she'd need to keep it brief.

Ham couldn't determine from the expression on Poppy Hartman's face what her decision was, and he found that fascinating. She was matching him, stare for stare, and that also interested him since he'd been told his stares could be intimidating. That was rarely his intention and it was not in this instance.

Poppy wasn't surprised when Ham didn't speak first, and she knew if she didn't say something soon the man would disappear inside. "You're hired."

Hell, *yeah*. The experiment would continue. He thought about what he needed to accomplish inside; some painting, including the cabinets, and the wood flooring. "Saturday okay?"

"That works." She was about to turn around but she just had to know, no matter how nosy she was being. "It appears Linc moved out and you moved in and I hope that isn't the way you operate because that isn't going to fly with me." Did she just see the man's lips move amongst all that beard, almost as if he were trying not to smile? Because his eyes certainly appeared to be smiling. "That shows an inordinate amount of trust on Linc's part, and maybe he knows you very well, but I don't."

"Linc's my brother." He saw her eyes widen and he was surprised Linc hadn't mentioned it to her.

"Where's Linc?"

"My place."

"You traded homes while you're working? Not that it's any of my business."

"Correct." Realizing how much he was enjoying the conversation, he knew he'd better get inside, and he stood. "Back to work."

Correct they had traded homes or correct it was none of her business? Either way, she needed to go home. "Same for me. See you Saturday."

And maybe it would be before Saturday if Ham timed it right. He'd caught a glimpse of her the past few nights on her walk to the water for her brief swims, and each time he'd asked himself when he was going to take a swim himself.

Maybe tonight was the night.

Chapter 13

Ham made two trips to Home Zone after lunch, the first for the wood flooring, and the second for the tiles. He stacked the boxes of wood in Linc's living room, but the tile storage required some thought. Standing by the bed of his truck, he eyed Poppy Hartman's house, picturing her living room. There was enough space to put them down against a wall for a few days. Cutting open the plastic, he pulled out a length of tile and headed for her cottage.

Poppy hadn't expected to see Ham this soon. Noticing what he was carrying, she smiled and pushed open her screen door. "Is this mine? It's gorgeous."

Ham stepped in once he realized both he and the tile were welcome and he handed the length to her.

"It's heavy, isn't it?" she asked.

He gestured to what he considered a suitable location. "All right if I stack the boxes there?"

"Sure."

"Did you choose your grout?"

"I didn't. I can go get that now. How much do I need?"

"Start with fifty pounds."

"Is that in a bag or a box or a plastic bucket?" Was she going to be able to lift a fifty pound whatever, which would be awkward and bulky?

"Get the premixed in a bucket. Aim for a color that's close to the darkest color on the tile. You don't want it to be noticeable."

"Okay," Poppy said. "You have all the tiles in your truck? Do you want me to bring them over here?"

She thought he expected her to haul them? "I've got it, if you'll let me use your driveway."

"Of course. Thank you."

"I'll get the grout once you tell me what color you want," Ham said.

"Really?"

"That's how it works." How the hell did Ham know how it worked? He'd never done anything other than gutting and rebuilding his own house, and that had been a learning curve he hoped never to live through again.

"Thank you. I'll go to Home Zone as soon as the tile is in a pile."

Ham headed over to get his truck, the image of her smile stuck in his head. As he climbed inside, he reminded himself this was an experiment and only an experiment, one intended to someday make his life more fulfilling. Or at least less lonely.

Poppy joined Ham beside his truck once he'd backed it up to her Jeep, and she watched him lift the first box, noting with amazement the way his biceps and triceps rose to the occasion. *Wow*. She'd propped her screen door open, and once he was inside her cottage, she reached for the next box, easing her fingertips under it and readying for the anticipated weight. Except she could barely even move the thing, let alone raise it enough to get a grip. Which was a moot point since she'd never be able to carry it. "*Hell's bells*. How can anyone pick these up?"

"I'll get them."

Poppy hadn't heard Ham return, and she stepped back and out of his way. "How much do those weigh?" She watched him heft the next one as if it were a gallon of milk.

"Enough to get the job done." Ham held back his smile until he was inside. He had to admire the fact she'd even tried, and he wondered if she thought she was going to "help" with the tiling or shingling.

Poppy returned to her living room since she wouldn't be of any help outside, and she watched as the pile of tile grew along with her excitement. Her floors were going to be absolutely beautiful. The ceiling and walls were already gorgeous, and once the new floors were in, she didn't know how she'd ever be able to leave her cottage. It was such a shame Couril didn't let their employees work remotely. She pictured herself on her deck in the sun as she worked on her laptop, or in her living room on less than perfect days. She really needed to get some chairs for her deck. *Today*. While she was at Home Zone she could check out what they had.

Ham came in with yet another bunch of tile and set it down.

"That's it," he said.

Something had occurred to her earlier, and she wasn't going to be shy about bringing it up. She hadn't been shy about anything else. "We need to shake on this."

"Shake?" Ham put his hands on his hips.

She extended her right hand. "You know, seal the deal. Neither one of us signed anything, so we need to shake to make it official." Ham wiped his hand on his shorts before gripping hers, his hand feeling huge and strong and warm. With a few callouses. A man's hand. "Thank you. I'll go see about the grout now."

As Ham drove back to Linc's driveway, he wondered if he should have suggested going to Home Zone with Poppy so they could wrap up the flooring supply situation.

Probably not a good idea. Walking into Linc's cottage, he thought about the feel of Poppy's hand in his.

No. Not a good idea at all.

POPPY HAD NO TROUBLE choosing the grout. The difficult part was trying to lift the bucket. Ham had said he'd get it once she made her decision about the color, but since she was at the store already it seemed silly for the man to make another trip. Maybe if she found a helpful employee she could handle it herself.

Half an hour later she was in the Jeep, gazing back at her purchases; a bucket of grout, and three plastic deck chairs, one red, one white, one blue. She'd even been able to find a little white table which would hold at least a few drinks. Maybe even a plate.

Reaching home, she knew she had to ask Ham to carry in the bucket, but it didn't have to happen right now. She could keep it in the Jeep until he came over to start work on her cottage so she wouldn't interrupt him.

Carrying the chairs one at a time, she got them settled on her deck. She appreciated the fact they were stackable, and in the winter, she'd store them in her little shed. They looked patriotic and pretty lined up on her deck. Deciding she'd put it off long enough, she returned to the Jeep for one more try to lift that bucket.

Ham was painting, "Hungry Like the Wolf" entertaining him from his phone on the kitchen counter, when he heard doors slamming, and he headed for the front door to take a look around. Seeing Poppy carrying a red Adirondack chair toward her deck, he thought about offering to give her a hand but she seemed to have the situation under control. Deciding it was time for a break, he stayed where he was, watching her carry a white chair out back before she returned to the Jeep's tailgate. Whatever was in there was giving her a hard time, and he was out the door before he had time to rethink his decision.

"Need a hand?"

Poppy hadn't noticed Ham approaching, but his timing was perfect. "Yes. This grout is getting the better of me."

"How'd you get it in the Jeep?" Ham asked.

"The nice man at Home Zone did it for me." When Ham lifted it as easily as he had the tiles, she said, "Thank you." Opening her front door, she held it for him and he set the bucket down beside the tile.

Ham could have said he was supposed to get the grout, but he kept the thought to himself, and he did appreciate she'd taken the trouble to get it home. "Anything else?"

"That's it. Thanks again." Poppy followed Ham the three steps to the door and watched him walk over to Linc's yard before she turned away to decide what she wanted to do next.

In minutes she was pulling out a section of tile and laying it over the old carpeting, just to see what her floor would look like in a few days.

Gorgeous. It would be absolutely gorgeous.

Chapter 14

It was time for a break. Poppy knew she deserved a break. Anyway, dinner was over, the day was perfect, and she was going to swim, then watch the sun setting over the water. The neighboring beaches were quiet at this hour, and she glanced next door, wondering what was happening at Linc's cottage. And how late Ham would be working on whatever he was doing.

Linc was incredibly lucky to have a brother who was willing to do all his updating. She thought about them trading houses while the work was ongoing and she wondered where Ham's house was. Was he in Belvedere? Was his house on the beach, either Surf Drive or one of the other beaches in town?

If Ham wasn't such a private man she could ask him every question she had about both him and Linc, too. But he was a private man. And she didn't typically pry into anyone's life because it was none of her business. Although lately she'd been doing quite a bit of prying.

She did enjoy coming up with her own answers to her questions about others and creating back stories for everyone she found interesting. Ham definitely qualified as interesting. Ham Wheeler, if he shared Linc's last name, but she wasn't going to assume. And she wouldn't assume Ham was his actual first name, either, but she supposed it was possible. Except the man had too much ... too much *presence* to be name just *Ham*.

Changing into her tankini and grabbing her blue towel, she went out the back door and looked toward the sun, now hanging low in the sky. She felt so grateful for what she had as she dropped her towel on her very own beach at her very own beach cottage. Living here was a dream come true. Not her biggest dream, but one day she'd find that special someone who not only said he wanted children but actually did.

Ham heard the door close at Poppy's cottage and he watched from Linc's deck as she strode to the water, then made a smooth dive under the waves. He thought about the day Linc had joined her in the water, the two of them riding the waves side by side.

Maybe his brother had better sense than he did. Returning inside, he headed for the bedroom to change his clothes.

Poppy saw Ham on the deck in nothing but gray boardshorts, a striped towel gripped in one hand, his eyes on the water.

Hell's bells and wishing wells ...

She told herself she shouldn't be surprised by the breathtaking sight of those shoulders, arms, and legs, not to mention the smattering of dark hair on his chest, but she felt blindsided by so much skin. And he was muscular, but not excessively so. Only in a very attractive way. But of course he'd need muscles to be lifting heavy tiles and buckets of grout and other things.

And maybe even a girlfriend. Who knew what kinds of fun things he would get up to with a girlfriend? Just because she hadn't seen Ham with a girlfriend didn't mean there wasn't one. Then he took a dive only feet away from her and she wondered if he would surface right in front of her.

Ham thought if he were twenty years younger, he could rise out of the waves and take Poppy in his arms, maybe slowly turn her in a circle, maybe kiss her a few times so they'd taste the salt water on each other's lips.

But he was thirty-five, not fifteen, and he knew better than to behave like a fifteen-year-old, so he'd make sure to give her plenty of room. Surfacing a safe distance away, he told himself keeping an eye on her was acceptable since she wouldn't want him to bump her.

Poppy wasn't going to just float there without saying anything. That would be ridiculous. The man was only a few feet away from her, and there was no one else around. "So why don't you have your company name on your truck so you get more business?"

"What company name?" Ham maneuvered himself a little closer to Poppy. All in the interests of hearing her better.

"You know. Your construction work. Your remodeling or renovating or whatever you call it."

"There's no company."

"Well, there's you and your tools," she said.

He wondered if the truth would mean she'd change her mind. Take back her handshake. "I'm no professional."

She tried to maintain eye contact with him, but with the rise and fall of the waves, it was challenging. "If you work and get paid for it, I'd call you a professional." The way he'd shingled Linc's cottage certainly looked professional, and she'd had several opportunities to notice.

"You're my first paying customer." When he saw her frown, he guessed what was coming next.

Poppy moved her arms around so she could put her feet down in the shifting sand. "Okay, I'm not asking for your life story, but I saw the way you shingled Linc's cottage, and I know you're painting and doing his floors and who knows what else. If this isn't what you do for a living, then where did your renovating skills come from?"

"Summer jobs when I was in school."

That made sense. But how did he get and maintain those muscles? And really, was that important right now? "Okay. And I'm not asking for your resume, but what have you been working on lately, other than Linc's cottage?"

Not asking for his resume. He looked at Linc's place, trying not to smile. Maybe he should email his resume to her. "I bought an old farmhouse a few years ago and did a full gut reno, except for the wiring and plumbing. The professionals handled that."

She pictured Ham swinging a sledge hammer at walls, because that's what people always used on home improvement shows, and she wondered for half a second if his nickname was Ham because he used a hammer. No. That was a stupid idea. "What is Ham a nickname for? If Ham is a nickname."

"Hamilton."

"Hamilton suits you." She lifted her legs and floated again, looking up at her cottage with its old, grayed shingles, picturing it with new fresh ones. It was going to be so beautiful.

"Is yours a nickname?"

She was amazed he'd ask and that he'd even want to know. "Yes. For Penelope."

"Works better."

"Poppy has fewer syllables."

"You work remotely?" he asked.

"No, I took two weeks off to fix up my cottage, then I'll go back." He hadn't asked, but why not tell him? When would she ever catch him being this talkative again? "I work at Couril." When he tilted his head, she said, "You've heard of it?" Since it was the largest employer in the county, this wasn't a surprise.

"What department?" He'd never seen Poppy Hartman in the building, and even though the company had eight floors, he thought he should have seen her at least once.

"In Customer Support."

"I'm in Business Operations."

"You are? I've never seen you there. Not that I go to Business Operations, but that's amazing." Ham was staring at her as if he were trying to place her face. Well, good luck to him, since she never went to Couril looking like a wet cat, her makeup all washed off, hair wet, messy, and stringy. *Wow.* Hamilton Wheeler at Couril? "Is your last name Wheeler?"

"Yes."

Poppy shook her head. "I haven't heard of you, but there are about a thousand of us working there, so that's not unusual." When a sudden gust of wind came up she shivered. "I'm cold, so I'm going in. Good night." She didn't wait for Ham's response, just flipped over and swam to the shallows.

Ham watched Poppy leave the water and retrieve her towel, wrapping it around her until only her calves and feet were visible, then when she reached her deck to finish drying herself, he looked away.

Poppy Hartman at Couril? He wasn't sure how he felt about that.

Chapter 15

Thursday and Friday nights, when Ham had seen Poppy heading for the water from his post at the kitchen window, he'd stayed where he was until she finished playing in the waves and was back on the beach, wrapping herself in either the striped or the blue towel, then he waited until she was inside before he went onto the deck to watch the sun set. He'd positioned the chair so he'd be less visible from Poppy's deck because he knew she'd be outside soon for the same reason he was there.

He was going to miss watching the sun set over the water when he was back in his own place.

He was also going to miss seeing Poppy taking a swim every night.

He hadn't joined her after the first night. But he'd seen her the past two nights.

His experiment had been a success in some respects and an epic fail in others. Working in her cottage, so close to her, for the next who the hell knew how many days, was going to be more of a challenge than he'd imagined the day he offered to give her the quotes. He had no choice now, so he'd finish her jobs and that would end all contact with her.

In order to finish, however, he needed to first begin. Walking across Linc's new wood floors on Saturday morning, he wondered when his brother would be coming over to check out the changes. He'd texted Linc to say he'd be at Poppy's for most of the day, but he hadn't heard back.

Since the weather was cooperating, he'd start on the outside. His truck bed still held the shingles he'd picked up the day before, and he was going to park in Poppy's driveway. It would keep the work area neater. Adding the barrel and his tools to the truck bed, he drove over and walked to her front door.

Poppy heard the truck in her driveway and knew who it was, and after drying her hands on a towel she met Ham at her door. She'd guessed when he'd waited to swim on Thursday and Friday nights until after she'd gone inside that her interrogation on Wednesday night had been too intrusive. She wasn't going to make that mistake again. "Good morning."

"Morning. Starting the shingling now. All right if I leave the truck behind your Jeep?"

"Yes. I'm not going anywhere."

He nodded. "I'll get to work."

"Thank you." She watched him return to his truck then she left the screen door. She'd be keeping an eye on him today, but it would be subtle. Or possibly screamingly obvious, such as when she went to check on the transformation of her cottage. The day was already another hot one, and she knew Ham would be sweltering out there in his white tee shirt and khaki shorts and work boots.

Which was why she had a pitcher of ice water to keep him hydrated. There was nothing intrusive about giving a man a few cups of ice water. She wouldn't ask him any personal questions, she'd just hand him the cup. She didn't even have to speak to him if he didn't seem to be in a speaking frame of mind.

Ham wondered if he should hope for rain so he'd be forced to head inside to start tearing up the old carpet. Then he decided the weather was going to do what it always did, which was remain unpredictable, and he'd adapt as needed.

He wondered what Poppy was doing inside. Maybe it was better that he was outside today, because keeping his eyes off her in that pink tank top and those little cutoffs would have been a serious struggle. With that body, and its tantalizing hills and valleys, she could distract even a man who was determined not to be distracted.

Prying off another shingle and dropping the pieces into the barrel, he told himself to think about something else. The Sox. The Pats. The Bruins. The Celts. Any team. Hell, even the Orioles or the Rays. Think about the last home series when the Sox were swept.

He glanced at the sky, a vivid blue today, reminding him of Poppy's bathing suit. *Hell.* He pulled out his phone and tapped the screen, telling himself to focus on the music. First up was "She Drives Me Crazy", and he shook his head. Just great.

Focus on shingles.

Count the number of pieces that splinter off.

Think about how many nails you're going to need.

How many trips to the dump you'll have to make.

"Ice water?"

He was startled, but managed not to drop the pry bar when Poppy spoke from beside him, a big plastic cup in her hand, ice cubes jostling. "Yeah. Thanks."

She wanted to stay and watch him drink it down, but she turned toward her back door, reminding herself about all the housework she still had to do. And the fact Ham didn't want her hanging around and asking personal questions. He was still ripping off the shingles so there was nothing exciting to see. Just the paper underneath the old shingles. Tar paper, if she wasn't mistaken. It was some kind of water barrier, anyway. A barrier that would protect her house so she didn't have to think about shingling again for about thirty years.

Pulling open her back door, she tried to picture herself in thirty years, at sixty-five. Would she have a husband? Children? Grandchildren?

Then she thought of the years with Connor. Years that she'd thought were building to what she'd always wanted; a husband and children. So Connor had lied about wanting children. There was no point being bitter. Bitterness was just as destructive as anger.

Ham was prying off a shingle next to a window when he caught movement inside. Poppy had a hand to her forehead, sorrow all over her face, and he paused, wondering if he should ask if she was all right.

Putting down the pry bar, he thought about knocking on her door, asking her for more water so he could check on her, then she moved and stood taller, her expression changed. She wasn't smiling, but the sorrowful look had passed. He looked away and pried off another shingle.

Chapter 16

Hungry. That's what her problem was. She was hungry. Poppy opened the refrigerator to take inventory, making a decision and pulling out ingredients. Maybe she was way off base, but she was going to do it anyway. There was some shade on the side of the house Ham was working on, and she wondered if he'd planned his work around the direction of the sun. She wrapped the sandwiches and put them on a platter, then went outside.

This time Ham saw when Poppy was coming, and his glance took in the food and her smile.

"I made turkey and roast beef sandwiches. You are under no obligation to take them, but if you choose to take them, you are under no obligation to eat them here, either on the deck or in the kitchen or right here. I have chairs so we won't have to sit on the sand."

Ham had been watching Poppy as she explained the situation, wondering if he'd be able to hide his smile this time. "We?"

"Right," she said. "I didn't mean to imply my presence was required, since you would probably prefer to eat alone. Possibly in Linc's kitchen."

"Are you eating, too?"

"Yes."

"Your deck. Just going to wash up first."

"I'll see you on the deck, then." Poppy walked back, bringing the plate inside. She wasn't sure what Ham considered washing up, but she wasn't going to leave food outside longer than it needed to be there. Pouring two cups of ice water, heavy on the ice, she got a second plate for her own sandwich, then added a bowl of grapes to the collection. Washing her hands again, she kept an eye out the window while she second-guessed her decision.

Lunch with Poppy Hartman. It hadn't been on Ham's schedule or even as a G-rated intro to a fantasy, yet it was about to happen. He texted Linc saying he was going to be busy for the next half hour, so if he wanted to come over Ham wouldn't be available. Linc might ask what was going on, but it was possible he wouldn't even see the text until lunch had been wrapped up.

After he'd washed his hands, face, neck and applied another couple layers of Speed Stick, he headed over, and by the time he reached Poppy's deck, she was there. "Appreciate this, but it's not necessary."

"I know, but I had the food, so I went for it. Maybe I was just hoping to keep your nose to the grindstone so my cottage will be transformed that much sooner. Also, I didn't ask how you felt about mayo, mustard, and pickles, so I left them off but they're all right inside and I'm happy to bring them out. Or you can come inside to add them."

Ham unwrapped the first of the two sandwiches, a roast beef, and took a bite. Food eaten outside always tasted better. Food eaten only a few feet away from Poppy Hartman would always taste best.

"We need pickles. This is too plain." Poppy stood. "Pickles and what else? Mustard? I might have some hot sauce."

"Mustard and pickles would be great. Thanks."

Poppy wished she'd bought a second table, but she pulled the third chair closer and set the tray on it. Once the condiments and silverware were on the table, she said, "Go crazy." She waited for Ham to doctor up his sandwiches, then she added a few slices of pickle to her own. "Yum. That makes all the difference."

"It's good." Ham took another bite, keeping his eyes on the water.

After lunch, Poppy wished it was time for a swim, but she could hardly go in while Ham was working so hard. Instead she stayed inside, deciding to read for a while.

It wasn't long before the hammering started up, and she was excited Ham had reached what she considered the important part of the job. No matter how badly she wanted to watch, she was going to wait before she went out to see what was happening.

She was well into her book when she heard male voices, and she looked out to see Linc was with Ham. Keeping her finger between the pages, she walked outside to say hello. Linc was in his board shorts again, the familiar towel around his neck, and he gave her a wave.

"Hey, Poppy. You feel like swimming?"

Poppy hadn't intended to look at Ham, and when she saw him watching her, she met Linc's eyes again. "Hi. I go later but you have fun."

"See you." Linc waved again, then he headed for the water. Poppy met Ham's eyes again, instantly wishing she hadn't.

"You can go with him. You don't have to stay here." Ham turned his head, wishing he could take back his words. She didn't need him to tell her what she could do. Picking up another shingle, he put it in place before giving the nail a good pounding. He wished she would say something. Or go inside.

Poppy wondered about the look on Ham's face, but staring at him wasn't going to supply her with any answers, so she went inside. Clearly the man needed a drink. Returning outside less than a minute later with another cup of ice water, she extended it, saying nothing.

Maybe he'd take it.

Maybe he'd ignore her.

Maybe he'd tell her he didn't need her to keep him hydrated.

"Thank you, Poppy." Ham took the red cup from her hand, then drank it down, leaving the ice cubes to chew on once she left him alone again. Breaking their eye contact, he looked at Linc floating on the waves. Maybe the kid was smarter than all of them, taking the time to cool off. He watched Poppy return to the deck. Probably to head inside, maybe to change her clothes and join Linc.

Thank you, Poppy. That was the first time Ham had said her name. He pronounced it differently than most people did, and the sound of it had taken her by surprise. Which must have been why she hadn't been able to stop staring at him. And getting caught. Once she was back in the living room, she turned on her music again. "Red Red Wine" was playing. *Perfect.*

Ham tapped his phone, ready for some music. When "Take on Me" started, he wondered if the fates were laughing at him again.

FINISHING UP THE LAST shingle, Ham stood back to check his work. Straight lines, no holes, all was in order. He heard someone behind him and turned to see Linc, now changed into shorts and a tee shirt, his hair still wet from the swim.

"Hey, can I take you out for dinner, Ham? Maybe we can ask Poppy."

Ham took Linc by the arm, walking him away from the cottage's open windows, hoping Poppy hadn't heard Linc's voice. "Thanks, but I need to keep at this."

"You have to eat."

"I'll eat later."

"Did you have lunch?"

"Yeah. Poppy made sandwiches."

"Maybe I should ask if she wants to go out with me. We can bring you back something so you don't have to stop working."

Ham stared at his brother, wondering why Linc didn't see that was a terrible idea.

"I'll ask Poppy," Linc said.

Watching Linc head for the front door, Ham wondered if he should have said something. Like what? Don't force me to spend more time with her than I have to because my experiment is backfiring?

The doorbell startled Poppy, and she jumped off the couch. "Hi, Linc. How's the water?"

"Great. Listen, I wondered if you wanted to go out for dinner. Ham refuses to stop working, probably until the fireflies come out."

Go out to *dinner*? With *Linc*? "Oh, thanks for asking, Linc, but I thawed something and I need to cook it. You have fun."

"Can I bring you something? I'm bringing some for the workaholic out here."

"That's really kind, but I'm all set. Enjoy your dinner."

"You, too."

She watched Linc jump down the two steps and disappear around the corner before she returned to the couch. He was nice to have asked, but every time she spoke with him he seemed to have gotten even younger.

"You two are no fun," Linc said to Ham, his voice lowered. "I'll bring you back whatever you want. What do you feel like?"

Poppy had refused, had she? Why that pleased him, Ham couldn't say. At least not in his current state of denial. "Surprise me, Linc. I'll eat whatever you bring back."

"You got it."

Chapter 17

When Poppy became aware of the silence later, she checked the windows to see Ham walking over to Linc's cottage. Linc was on the deck with a brown paper bag, and she was pleased she hadn't ruined anyone's plans because she said no to Linc. It was good Ham was finally off his feet after all the hours he'd put in today. She loved the look of the new shingles, and was so pleased with Ham's work and she couldn't wait to see what he did with the flooring.

Giving the ground beef one more stir, she turned off the burner and drained the pasta. Glancing over at Linc's deck, she saw the guys were eating out of white cartons, and it instantly made her wish she were having Chinese food, too. Instead it would be American chop suey. As soon as she dumped the pasta into the beef and drowned it all in tomato sauce.

Then she could decide if she wanted to take a swim. Once there was no one on the deck next door.

"THE PLACE LOOKS GREAT, Ham," Linc said.

Ham had his eye on Poppy's cottage. "Yeah."

"Don't sound so excited. Something wrong with the roast duck? Tastes all right to me," Linc said.

"Nothing wrong with it."

"Is all this work wearing you out? I know you're used to sitting at a desk all day, and this must be tiring."

Ham shifted his focus to his smart ass kid brother. "I think I can handle it."

"Maybe you need to spend more time in that water." Linc aimed his thumb over his shoulder, then took a bite of fried rice.

"Once I finish I will. How are you doing living out in the woods?"

"You kidding? Your place is a mansion compared to mine," Linc said.

"You have a whole ocean out your back door. I'd call it even."

"You want to take a swim after dinner? Prove you haven't forgotten how to have fun?"

Ham pictured Poppy joining them, urged by his brother. "After the sun sets."

"I'm coming over with some of my buddies tomorrow afternoon. Show them my place."

"I'll stay out of your way."

Linc laughed. "I want them to meet you since you're the brother with all the handy skills. You're the one who made my place what it is."

"You painted it."

"Well, I guess I did do *some* of the work."

Ham smiled. "You need to try harder with that humble act."

Ham was able to convince Linc not to linger after dinner, then he headed back to put in some more time on the shingles. First he made a stop at Poppy's front door, giving it a couple knocks.

Poppy had known Ham would return since he'd left his tools behind, so seeing him on her front porch wasn't a surprise. "Hello."

"Okay if I put in another hour or two?"

"Of course." She thought he would have had enough by now, but knew better than to say that. He gave her a nod, then he was off the porch and back to work.

Later she'd swim. Linc had left, and she doubted Ham would be swimming tonight. Plus, if he were working on the front of the house, he wouldn't even see her in the water.

It had been a good plan until she stepped onto her deck in her tankini and came face to face with Ham. *Hell's bells.* His hands were on a pile of shingles and his eyes were all over her. But only for a second, then his eyes met hers. His tee shirt was damp with sweat and there were beads of sweat on his brow. Of course he'd be sweating. He'd been working for hours. "I'm not trying to tell you what to do, but you've accomplished an impressive amount of work today and maybe you should take a swim and relax the rest of the night. The shingles will wait."

That hadn't been an invitation, and he wouldn't take it as one. "Maybe I should." After she nodded and stepped off her porch, again dropping her towel halfway to the water, he put the shingles down and went to gather his tools.

Poppy submerged herself, the cold water feeling as shocking as it always did, but she was instantly refreshed. She hoped Ham would swim, even if it was later.

After a few minutes of floating, she noticed a trio of preschoolers making sandcastles at a neighboring beach, then she looked around and saw Ham on Linc's deck, again in the gray board shorts. He stepped off the deck, his eyes again on her, and she knew what he'd do next. When he surfaced a few feet from her, he stretched out so he could stay afloat.

"Isn't this better than working?" she asked.

"Doesn't pay the bills."

He was looking toward the little kids she'd been watching, and his lips curved up in a smile. She looked again to see one of the kids pour a bucket of water on another, and the shout of outrage made her grin. "What does Linc think of his new floors? You finished them, right?"

"They're finished, and he likes them. You didn't want the wood?"

"I was worried about the sand scratching them. Maybe the tile is just as scratchable, I don't know. But I'm happy with my choice."

"They'll look good."

"And maybe the sand will be easier to sweep up from the tile. It's too bad the cottage doesn't have an outdoor shower so the sand wouldn't matter as much."

"You could always dump a bucket of water over you like that kid just did," he said.

She laughed. "Maybe I'll keep a bucket on the deck for that. How much time did you take off? To help Linc? And now me?"

"Two weeks."

"How do you want me to pay you? We didn't discuss that. I can give you cash or a check since I'm assuming you don't take American Express. Which is fine since I don't have an American Express."

"No black card?"

"Pretty amazing, I know. Especially when you see the size of my cottage and my impressive three-year-old Jeep." She looked at him and caught another smile. It was slight, but it was there.

"I think you do all right for yourself."

"You know what? I do. I love my cottage and living here right on the beach. I know hurricanes are always a potential threat, but I still want to be here."

"Mother Nature is always going to win, especially when you live this close to the ocean. You paint and shingle and replace the roof and seal the windows so your place is tight but the maintenance is ongoing and it never ends. If you stop taking care of it for five or six years you can lose everything you've put into it. And as you said, there's the threat of hurricanes and tidal surges, and with the low elevation, Mother Nature always wins."

Poppy stared at Ham, who was looking toward the shore, maybe at her cottage, maybe at Linc's. She couldn't argue with anything he'd said because it was true. Sadly. "I'm guessing your own house isn't on the beach."

"It's in the woods."

"Which kind of goes along with that beard." When he met her eyes, she said, "I think you know what I mean. Have you always worn a beard?"

Ham returned his eyes to Poppy's cottage, part of his brain thinking about where he'd start in the morning, another part wondering how much he thought Poppy needed to know. None of it, really. Still ... "It's been a year."

"Do you mean 'it's been a year' as in a really awful year or you've had the beard for a year?"

"Both." He stood in the waist-deep water. Staying here with Poppy was probably not a good idea, and when he felt a hand on his arm he looked at Poppy, who'd stood next to him.

"That was rude of me, and I apologize, Ham. I'll go in so you can stay out here."

He studied her, the way her wet hair was curling around her face, regret in her eyes, as the waves buffeted her. When a particularly strong wave hit her, she lost her footing and he gripped her upper arms to steady her. "How about your year, Poppy? How has it been?"

"Better now, but let's just say things really didn't work out the way I'd believed they were going to and that's time I'll never get back."

"No sense wasting more time thinking about it." He knew he should take his hands off her, but he wanted to pretend she needed him to keep her from being knocked over.

"You're right. And most days I don't let myself waste more time."

When Ham felt her shiver, he released her. "Time to go in."

"I agree." She turned for the shore and swam beside him until they reached the shallows. "I feel better, and I hope you cooled off. And I won't ask you any more personal questions."

"You can ask any question you want. And cash or check work."

She wrapped up in her towel and they separated. She thought about the feel of his strong hands on her arms, and she sent a few more glances at his back as he walked to Linc's.

Maybe she would ask more questions.

Maybe he'd answer.

Maybe he'd ask some of his own.

Maybe she'd answer, too.

Chapter 18

Ham realized on Sunday morning he should have checked with Poppy the night before about how early he could begin working. Taking his iced tea out to Linc's deck after breakfast, he gazed over at Poppy's deck, foolishly hoping she'd appear so he could ask. Movement in the water caught his attention, and he saw a woman gracefully rising out of the waves. Brunette, curvy, and streaming water. Poppy. He put down his drink and stepped off the deck, striding toward her. "You shouldn't swim alone."

Poppy stared at Ham, then wrapped herself in the towel, keeping her eyes on his. He'd never frowned at her like this before. "I don't go into deep water. You've seen where I go. But I appreciate your concern."

"Are you swimming every morning?" He hadn't noticed her until today, but maybe his timing was off.

"Today was the first day. You don't have to be concerned."

"If you're going in early, will you tell me?"

"You want to swim then, too?" That was a good idea for a couple of reasons, even if there was the little matter of her starting to think he was a really, really nice guy when she wasn't in the market for a guy of any kind, but he'd only be working around her cottage for maybe three or four more days, then he'd go back to his own house and she'd never see him again.

He wondered if she imagined she was goading him, then he realized she wouldn't. She wasn't childish or snide. "I'll swim with you."

"Good," she said. "Then we'll both have a swim buddy. Are you coming over today?"

"As soon as you say it's all right."

"It's all right." She walked up the beach to her deck, smiling. The man could only benefit from more swimming and less working. It was summer in Belvedere and he should be enjoying it. Drying off her feet to minimize the amount of sand she'd be tracking in, she thought about Ham's bucket on the deck idea. She just might do it.

Then she remembered a story her friend, Kristin, had told her about her own childhood, when her grandfather used to take her and her sisters to the beach when they were little, and before he let the girls back into his car, he'd sit them down and use a paint brush to dust all the sand off them.

Poppy thought it had been an ingenious idea, and she still felt that way. A paint brush beat a bucket of water for tidiness any day, and she had a small paint brush in the house that she hadn't even used. Maybe she'd hammer a nail into a shingle by the door so it would be handy.

She'd just stepped out of the shower when she heard the familiar sound of a shingle being torn off her cottage. Ham hadn't had a swim this morning, but she had a feeling he might have one later. His concern for her safety had surprised and pleased her, and was a reminder she should stop jumping to conclusions about people. Especially tall, strapping men with impressive beards and muscles who could carry heavy objects.

Pulling on a sundress because the day was already in the eighties, possibly touching ninety later, she went into the kitchen to get a drink and she refilled the pitcher of ice water to make sure Ham would be hydrated today. She needed to do some grocery shopping and knew the earlier she hit the store, the better. Taking her purse, she went out the back door, and there was Ham, tools in hand, with a reusable water bottle on the deck. "I'm off to the grocery store. Do you need anything?"

"No."

"There's ice water in the fridge for your refills if you want." She gestured to his water bottle.

"Thanks."

"Then I'll be off. See you in a bit."

"See you." He watched Poppy until she disappeared around the corner of the cottage, then heard her start the Jeep. He would be distraction-free for a while, and he needed to make better progress than he had been. Sliding on his safety glasses, he jammed the pry bar under the next shingle.

Poppy wondered what she should get for lunch for the next few days, in case Ham accepted another offering. She was well aware he might put his booted foot down and return to Linc's cottage, or even go out for something, but she'd be ready for anything.

It wasn't as if he was a stranger she'd hired from the internet. He was a colleague, although she hadn't known that originally. And he was the brother of her neighbor. They'd gone swimming together, they'd had a meal together. They were approaching friend-mode. She hoped Ham would consider her a friend, if not while he was working for her, then once he'd finished. She could certainly use a friend like Hamilton Wheeler. He, and also Linc, were helping her remember not all men were lying and self-serving.

Maybe someday she'd be able to find out what had made the past year a bad one for Ham. Maybe if she shared her story, he'd share his. Except she wasn't ready to share that story. Only her parents and Cara knew what had happened.

The thought reminded her she needed to invite them all over once her cottage was transformed. Her mother had called the night before admitting she was surprised Poppy hadn't called for any help, and Poppy had given her a summary of what had happened, then had promised to have them over soon, when everything was done.

She would call Cara once her bestie was home from vacation and they could plan a day for Cara to come over and enjoy the beach with her. Ham would be gone by then, and Poppy could decide how much she wanted to tell Cara about him. She knew Cara was all for Poppy getting back "out there" and finding a man "worthy" of her, but Poppy knew it was still too soon, even if she was in a much better frame of mind than she'd been in only weeks ago.

After shopping, she made her way through the slow moving traffic downtown, then along the seemingly always busy Surf Drive, finally pulling into her driveway. Ham hadn't driven his truck over today and she wondered why. Maybe once she was back in nosy-mode she'd ask him.

After hauling all her bags inside and putting everything in its places, all to the accompaniment of the sounds of hard work being performed right outside, she filled a cup with ice water and went out the back door to see Ham's bare chest as he struggled to pull on his tee shirt over what had to be sweat-soaked skin. An uphill battle, for sure. And unnecessary considering she'd seen the man's chest before. She'd turned her face away once their eyes had met because she didn't want him to be embarrassed, even though he had absolutely no reason to feel that way. Absolutely no reason.

Once his chest was covered, she said, "Two things. I brought you some water just in case, and if you're more comfortable with your shirt off, it's fine with me. I'll give you privacy and stay inside, and if you're interested, I'm making salad with chicken for lunch around noonish. You can take it to Linc's if you'd rather." Poppy spun around and returned inside, making it a point not to look out the kitchen door again. No matter how badly she wanted to see if Ham had pulled off his shirt again.

Ham eyed the door that had closed behind Poppy, processing what she'd said. Working shirtless had been a bad idea on every level, he knew that, but the heat had gotten to him. He picked up the cup of water, drinking it all down. Then he grabbed his bottle and stepped off the deck, pouring what was left onto his neck and back. It was a slight improvement, and he returned to the deck and picked up the pry bar again.

Chapter 19

Poppy had never before agonized over someone else sweating on her behalf, and she was having serious trouble dealing with her distress. Part of her knew she was being ridiculous, but the rest of her was scrambling with a solution. Checking the weather app on her phone, she saw rain was predicted overnight, with cooler temps for the next few days.

When lunch time rolled around, she prepared two salads, wondering if she'd end up eating them both because Ham didn't want the one intended for him. This would sadden her only because she wanted to make something a little easier for him, and she really had no control over anything else that might help him. Connor had never thought salad, AKA "rabbit food", could be considered a meal, and maybe Ham felt the same way.

Picking up the bowl and a napkin-wrapped knife and fork, she elbowed her way out the back door, immediately attracting Ham's attention. "Hello. Here is lunch, salad with chicken, as we discussed earlier. You may have it on the deck or in my kitchen, joined by me, or alone if you prefer, or you may take it to go and eat it anywhere you feel like eating it, or you may tell me you don't want this salad and I need to stop pestering you all the time. There's a selection of dressing in the fridge if you choose one of the first options, and there's plenty of ice water, which isn't dependent on any of the options I mentioned." Ham had kept his eyes on hers throughout her explanation, and his expression hadn't changed.

Maybe it wouldn't change.

Maybe he'd walk to Linc's cottage without a word.

"And no matter what you decide," she said, "it's really hot today but it's going to be cooler for a few days because of the rain coming tonight, and if you want to quit for the day right now, have lunch, then go swimming until you've cooled off, then take it easy the rest of the day, I am one hundred percent behind you."

Ham wondered if Poppy was in a management position at Couril. If she was, people would walk all over her. He'd spent some time since the night before wondering about Poppy's year and what had happened to her. Probably he'd never find out, but it wouldn't stop him wondering. Especially after what he'd seen through the window the day before. "Remind me what the third option was?" The look on her face was priceless. Then he smiled at her, and her smile returned. Damn, he felt that smile all the way to his soul. "Will you be swimming?"

"Will you?" she asked.

"Lunch on the deck, then swimming. Maybe working later when the sun's lower in the sky."

"Then more swimming after that?"

"Maybe. Give me five minutes?"

"Of course. I'll keep this in the kitchen until you're ready." *Hell's bells and wishing wells.* Poppy stepped into her kitchen, amazed by the outcome. She'd actually managed to convince the man.

As Ham returned to Linc's to take the quickest shower he'd ever had, he wondered when Linc and his friends would be coming over. Stripping off his sweat-soaked clothes, he turned on the shower, stepping in while the water was still cold, enjoying the feel of it on his skin for a couple seconds, then appreciating when it warmed. Lathering up, he hurried, only wanting to be clean, if not refreshed. There was time to cool off later when he and Poppy were in the ocean.

Poppy was definitely going to buy a bigger table for the deck. Maybe tomorrow since today was already booked, although if Ham left for Linc's house after a quick swim later, there would be time. Maybe he'd want to watch a ball game or something, just flop on the couch and relax, something she'd bet he hadn't done since he'd been staying at Linc's. He couldn't possibly have finished all the work he'd done and still have time to relax.

Watching Linc's cottage through the window, she saw the moment Ham stepped onto the deck, in different clothes, and she waited at the screen door, ready to welcome him. "Can you come in to check the salad dressing collection so I don't have to bring all five bottles outside?" When Ham stepped inside, she caught his scent, something fresh and clean. Gesturing to the lineup on the counter, she said, "Take your pick. Of the salads and the dressings."

"Appreciate this, Poppy. You don't have to feed me." Ham made his choice and shook the bottle before pouring it out. "Looks good."

"If this doesn't hit the spot, I have American chop suey, just what anyone would want when it's ninety degrees out."

"This will hit the spot just fine." He picked up the bowl and waited while Poppy added her dressing and put away the bottles. Seeing the two cups of water on the counter, he said, "Which is yours?"

"They're both untouched, so make your best choice." Once they were seated outside, she said, "I think I'm going to get a table with an umbrella. This sunny stuff every single day is really too much, isn't it?" She stared at Ham, wondering if what she'd just heard was a laugh, then she focused on her salad, giving it a good stir. Here she was, having another cozy lunch with the man doing work on her house. This wasn't the way it was supposed to be with people one hired and she wondered what her parents would think if they dropped in.

No, she really didn't wonder. If they found her on the deck with Ham, they'd assume the two of them were dating and things would get very awkward for Ham. And her. She hoped they didn't decide to drop in as a little surprise.

"Good salad," Ham said. Poppy had loaded it with chicken breast, and with the iceberg and romaine lettuce, and tomatoes and cucumbers, it was just right on a day this hot.

"Glad you think so." She took a drink of water, her eyes on the waves. She'd wondered as she'd imagined her whole lunch-with-Ham scenarios if Ham would make conversation during lunch and had decided she wasn't going to chatter if he wasn't. He was probably enjoying not hearing the sound of the shingles crunching and cracking and the hammer pounding the new shingles in. Right now, the sound of the waves and the kids' voices, with the occasional screech of a sea gull, were enough background noise.

Ham finished eating first, but he didn't move, didn't fidget, didn't make any kind of announcement. Poppy wondered how soon it would be before she stopped comparing the actions of every man she was around to Connor's behavior. It really needed to be soon.

As Ham watched the kids playing down by the water, colorful buckets and shovels all over the place, he thought about how easily he'd let Poppy talk him into not only having lunch with her but to knock off work for the day.

Then he wondered if he should be concerned about what else she might be able to talk him into. Or out of.

Chapter 20

"Thanks for lunch."

"You're welcome. You're going to swim now, right?"

"Yes."

Poppy waited until Ham had stood before she got up and gathered the lunch things. "I'll see you out there, then." She headed inside as Ham walked back to Linc's with his tools, then she pulled on her blue tankini yet again. She really needed to get another swimsuit before this one disintegrated. Dropping her towel near her deck, she strode through the hot sand, in a hurry to get into that water.

Ham walked down the beach, his eyes on Poppy's back as she made her usual dive under the waves. She'd done something different with her hair, tied it up. Maybe he wouldn't be seeing those wet ringlets framing her face today. He liked her hair, especially those ringlets, and he wondered what they would feel like wrapped around his fingers. Then he thought about what she would feel like wrapped around him.

Both of them naked.

It was a shame this wasn't a more secluded beach.

Although maybe it was better that it wasn't.

Diving in, he aimed for the area where Poppy was floating, knowing she'd seen him coming because she'd given him a little wave. "Feels good."

"It's perfect," Poppy said. "Isn't this better than working?"

"Guessing that's a rhetorical question."

"You guessed right." She liked the way Ham was floating near her again, but not too near. If anyone saw them, they wouldn't assume they were a couple. Just two people having a conversation. She really should start wearing her sunglasses, not only to protect her eyes, but so she could keep the objects of her scrutiny unaware. If Ham realized how often she looked at him he'd probably get irritated and stop swimming with her. "Do you prefer to be called Ham or Hamilton?" And this was another reason she should wear the shades, so when she rolled her eyes at the questions that seemed to leap out of her mouth without advance notice, Ham wouldn't see.

"Either."

"You seem too distinguished to be called Ham. You look more like a Hamilton."

He'd never been called distinguished in his life. "It's lucky my parents put Hamilton on the birth certificate."

"Is Linc short for Lincoln?"

"Yes."

"Are there any other siblings? And because I know you're dying to find out, I have one brother, who's older."

Ham smiled. "Good to know. We have a sister, Bonnie. She's the middle child."

As Poppy was trying to picture a younger Ham with a little sister, she saw three guys come out of Linc's house onto his deck, and it took her a couple seconds to realize one of them was Linc. "Linc is here."

"He said he'd be over with his buddies." Ham watched the trio, all in board shorts. Linc was blowing up a blue and white beach ball as they walked toward the water's edge.

After Linc introduced everyone, he and his friends began kicking the beach ball across the waves to each other as they floated on their backs. Poppy knew the peaceful interlude with Ham was over and she moved out of the way, preparing to make her exit. Ham remained close to the guys, and she thought once she went in, Ham might join their game.

After a few more minutes, she caught Ham's eye. "I'm going in."

"See you." Ham watched Poppy until the ball landed inches in front of his face, then he punched it toward Linc, wondering how long he wanted to stay in.

Poppy drank a glass of water at the kitchen window, pleased to see Ham had joined the game. Because of his thick beard, it was hard to tell from where she stood if he was smiling, but she hoped he was. It was just a silly kids' game, tossing a ball around, but the other guys were clearly enjoying it. She was feeling refreshed, but she needed to wash off the salt water, especially from her hair, and she headed in for a shower.

She was stretched out on her couch, reading, when she heard car doors slam, and she walked over to the door to see her parents coming up her walk. "Hello, there."

"Are we interrupting anything?" Lauren asked.

"No." Poppy pushed open the screen door and her parents stepped inside, both looking around.

"Nice job on the painting, Poppy," Nick said.

"This looks beautiful. And what do we have over here?" Lauren said.

"That's my flooring. Once Ham finishes with the shingles he's going to start on the floors."

"Ham?" Nick asked.

"Hamilton Wheeler. Ham. He's the brother of my neighbor, and he's already shingled that cottage, plus he did the floors and I don't know what else."

"He has good references?" Lauren asked.

"I've seen his work, so it's an eyewitness reference." Her parents didn't need to know Ham wasn't exactly a professional. She had every confidence in his work, and in him. "Did you see the shingles when you drove up?"

"No," Lauren said.

"Then let's step outside and take a look." Poppy led them to the back door, disappointed to see Ham had gone in already. None of the guys were there. Pointing to the shingles, she said, "See? He's started on the back wall, but he already finished the side over here." They all trooped off the deck and around to the side.

"This looks so nice, Poppy," Lauren said.

Nick put a hand on a couple of shingles. "Looks good."

"I can't wait until the whole cottage looks this great," Poppy said.

"We wanted to take you to dinner," Lauren said.

"I'd love that. You want to go now?"

"As soon as you're ready. Your father is starving."

Poppy grinned at her father, who did indeed look starving. When they walked out to her father's car, she saw only Ham's pickup in Linc's driveway, and she wondered what he was doing for dinner.

Ham watched Poppy leave in a silver Cherokee with a couple he presumed were her parents, and he wished he'd mentioned putting in another couple hours on the shingling. He was ready to get some work done, and sitting around wasting time when there was so much to do irritated him.

Grabbing his keys, he headed out to the truck. Dinner tonight would be prepared by hands other than his own. All he needed to do was decide what he felt like having. As he approached Big Fisherman, he saw a silver Cherokee parked there and he made a quick turn into the lot. Maybe Poppy would be inside and maybe she wouldn't.

Chapter 21

At the Big Fisherman, the pager buzzed on the table between them, startling Poppy. "I'll get the tray."

"Do you need help, honey?" Lauren asked.

"I've got it, Mom. Be right back." Pager in hand, she headed for the pickup counter. As she was handing the pager to the girl with the tray of food, she noticed Ham was ordering at the other counter, sliding his wallet into the back pocket of his shorts. Backing away from the counter, he turned his head and his eyes met hers. The smile he wore took her by surprise, until she told herself he would have smiled at the girl who took his order. As she was picking up the tray, he walked toward her.

"Hey, Poppy."

"Hi. I'm here with my parents." She gestured over her shoulder. "Do you want to join us?" Of course he didn't want to join them, and she should never have asked him.

Yes, he wanted to join them. But he wouldn't. "Mine's to go, but thanks. Any chance I can work on the shingles tonight? Maybe an hour."

"Really?"

"Yes."

"If you want to, then, sure."

"Can I get your number?" he asked. "In case you're out and I need to reach you?"

"Sure." She recited it, watching Ham add it to his phone before sliding it back into his pocket. "Maybe I'll see you later, then."

"Enjoy your dinner."

"You, too." She turned, wondering if her parents had seen her with Ham, but when she reached the table neither of them said anything. "Wow, this place is certainly busy tonight. Everybody must want seafood."

Ham waited near the pickup counter, staring into space. He had Poppy Hartman's number. What he thought he was going to do with that number he couldn't have said, but it was right on track for the experiment since he was going through the motions of a man who'd found himself drawn to a woman.

It was also practice for when he was ready to try again.

When he'd found a woman with the same dreams he had.

One who wanted what he wanted.

One who would love him the way he loved her.

For today, tomorrow, and forever.

He felt drawn to Poppy, yes, but she'd had ample opportunity to express feelings she might have for him and she hadn't. To her, he was just a guy doing work on her house.

He wished he understood what had caused those shadows he'd seen in her eyes. Maybe by the time he finished the jobs at her cottage he'd be ready to ask. And maybe she'd trust him enough to answer.

His attention was caught by the girl behind the counter, and she handed him his bag. Glancing around the crowded restaurant, he didn't see Poppy, so he headed toward the door, now in a hurry to get home so he could have dinner and get back to work.

And see Poppy again.

He ate as he drove, finishing before he even reached Linc's. Heading into the cottage, he washed his face and hands before he smeared his greasy fingerprints anywhere else, then he cleaned everything he'd touched before changing into work clothes and returning to Poppy's deck.

This felt right, being back to work. The evening was just as hot as the day had been, temperature-wise, but the sun was lower and he felt better from the swim. Knowing tomorrow would be cooler was more incentive to get something accomplished. Maybe he'd finish enough tonight to earn one of those smiles from Poppy that took his breath away. Maybe there'd be another great sunset they could watch together from her deck. Tapping his phone, he heard "Prove it All Night" playing, and he sang along with Springsteen as he worked.

Poppy thought about Ham working on the shingles, possibly right this minute. Then she thought about her parents wondering why a handyman, or whatever Ham considered himself, would be working on a Sunday night. If they came in the cottage with her, they'd hear what was going on, and they'd ask questions, questions she didn't want to answer. Not to mention if she introduced them all, her parents might see something in her eyes she didn't want them to see. "I had a nice swim today and I think it really tired me out." She looked at the backs of her parents' heads in the front seat, hoping they were getting her message. "I'm so glad I have another week off so I can sleep in tomorrow."

"I've got an early meeting tomorrow," Nick said.

"I won't keep you guys. Just drop me off if you want to get home. And thanks again for dinner. That was fun."

"We won't stay if you're tired, honey," Lauren said. "And I've got to go home and iron my outfit for tomorrow."

Poppy leaned forward and gave each of her parents a kiss on the cheek before jumping out of the back seat, getting inside, and giving them a big wave. Once they pulled away, she headed for the kitchen door.

When Ham heard the car door he paused his hammering, wondering if Poppy's parents would be visiting for a while. That would put an end to his shingling for the night. He didn't hear voices, but he kept his eyes on the back door, the pry bar in his hand, unmoving. Then Poppy was on the deck with him.

"Hi." Poppy looked over the back wall of her cottage. "This looks so great, Ham. It's a hundred percent better than before, and I'm so pleased with it."

"Still a long way to go."

"Only two more sides and a little of this side. But you're right. It's a lot of work for you."

"It takes longer than I want it to," he said, immediately wishing he hadn't.

"Doesn't everything?" She looked out over the water. "Look at that sunset, Ham. It's gorgeous. Maybe because it's supposed to storm."

She was right. The colors were rich and the sky was beautiful. "You okay with me working another half hour?"

"If that's what you want, then, sure. I'll be right inside." She'd rather sit and watch him, but she knew that was a terrible idea. Picking up her book again, she guessed she'd at least hear him working, even if she couldn't see him.

She was in the middle of turning a page when a clap of thunder made her jump, and she realized how much darker it had just gotten. Hurrying to the kitchen, she saw a zigzag of lightning flash and she pushed open the door and grabbed Ham, pulling on his arm, but he didn't budge. "We have to get inside, Ham. *Please.*" She tugged again, and this time he followed her. Then the deluge began, sheets of rain pounding down on the roof, the deck, everywhere. "Wow. Listen to that."

Ham looked from the deck to Poppy. "Pretty wild." Another bolt of lightning lit up the sky. "Quite a storm."

"I'm closing the door, then getting my windows."

"I'll get the door."

"Thanks. Are there windows open at Linc's?" she asked.

"Just cracked."

"Good, because I'm not letting you leave until the lightning has been over for thirty minutes." Poppy spoke over her shoulder as she went from window to window.

Ham walked into the living room, waiting for Poppy to finish running around. "Not letting me leave?" He expected she'd be smiling at him when she returned, but she wasn't.

"No. People die every year because they don't take lightning seriously. You are stuck here. Sorry."

That was a lie.

Poppy wasn't sorry at all.

Chapter 22

"Do you want to sit? I promise my couch is comfortable."

"My clothes are dirty," Ham said.

"They're fine, Ham." All the man had been doing was working with cedar shingles, not mud. When he shook his head and looked away, she knew she wasn't going to get him to change his mind. "Then can we sit at the kitchen table? I have a deck of cards." He met her eyes then. "Any game you want. Except poker because I've lost every game I've ever played. How about War? Or Go Fish?" She jumped when thunder crashed again. "Hell's bells, that sounded close. Do you want a drink before we start?"

"Nothing, thanks."

"I'll get the cards and you sit." Poppy wondered how Ham felt about her ordering him around tonight. Maybe she needed to ease up a little. Taking the cards from the drawer, then sitting, she was thankful when he sat across from her. "What do you think?"

"War."

"Perfect."

As the thunder and lightning did their thing, Poppy enjoyed their card games and she hoped Ham wasn't bored out of his mind. He seemed to be having some fun, but it was hard to tell with him. Every time she saw lightning she noted the time.

The storm gradually subsided, and it was after nine before she said, "That's thirty minutes since the last strike."

"You kicking me out now that I'm winning?" Ham was amused by the look on Poppy's face.

Ham joking? This was a first. Maybe potentially dangerous storms had that effect on him. "You stay as long as you want. And I believe I'm winning." When he reached across the table and scooped the cards out of her hands to add them to his, she laughed. "What's that called?"

"A draw." Ham neatened the cards and replaced them in their box. "Thanks for the entertainment."

"You're welcome. Even though I'm pretty sure I was going to win that hand."

"We'll never know, will we?" Ham headed for the back door to grab his tools.

"Let me get the light." Poppy tapped the switch for the deck lights, and Ham turned his head to look at her.

"Night, Poppy. See you in the morning."

"Good night."

As he walked through the wet sand back to Linc's place, Ham thought their night should have ended with a kiss. But kissing wasn't allowed in experiments. And kissing would only muddy the waters and leave him even more confused.

HAM PUT UP THE LAST shingle on Tuesday around dinner time, then he walked the perimeter of the cottage looking for anything that needed his attention. Once he was satisfied, he knocked on Poppy's front door.

Poppy knew Ham had been getting close because she'd checked his progress a couple of times that day when he'd made his trips to the dump with the barrels of old shingles. When she heard the knocking, she met him at the front door, knowing what he was going to tell her. "Hello."

"Want to walk around, make sure you're happy with the job?"

She knew she was happy with the job, but she stepped outside and followed him. "It looks beautiful, Ham. Like my cottage is in a giant ray of sunshine instead of a cloud. Are you going to charge extra because you had to work around those thorny beach roses?" She'd actually made him smile again. She looked carefully at his work because he was watching her and she wanted him to know she appreciated the time and care he'd taken. "I love it. Do you want me to give you a check now for everything? The shingles and the tiling?"

"Not until I finish."

Ham had refused her offer of lunch the past two days, and even though she'd been disappointed, she'd understood. She hadn't gone swimming Monday night because the weather had cooled, and tonight she'd probably skip it again. But she'd watch the sun setting. She didn't need company to sit and watch a sunset.

"Do you want the extra shingles stored in the shed?"

"Yes. I hope I never need them."

"I'll start the flooring in the morning. How early should I be here?"

"How does eight sound?"

"See you at eight."

After Ham and Poppy, but mostly Ham, had carried the extra shingles to the shed, he took his tools and left, and Poppy went into the cottage to make dinner. And call Cara to invite her over for Saturday so they could swim and have lunch.

Poppy needed Cara to meet Ham, then share her opinion of him. Poppy badly needed a second opinion. Maybe even some counseling.

Chapter 23

On Wednesday morning after Ham had removed the old carpeting and filled the two barrels he'd brought with him, Poppy, who'd been watching from the kitchen, asked, "Do you want me to bring those barrels to the dump?" Ham met her eyes then, a crooked smile on his lips.

"I've got it, Poppy."

"Then I'll get out of your way so you can do what you need to do. I'll be on the deck with my book if you need anything."

When he left with the barrels she returned to the living room, eying Ham's tools, wondering if she dared try removing the bedroom carpeting herself. No, she probably didn't dare. Nor did she want to try ripping up the linoleum floor in the kitchen. But maybe Ham could lay the tile right over that. It was flat enough.

Ham hadn't asked Lawson about going to Bud's on Monday night, wanting to keep it open in case Poppy wanted to swim. As it turned out, she hadn't. Now that he was working inside her cottage, she seemed to be everywhere he was. Even if she wasn't in his sight, she was constantly in his head, and he needed a change of scene. An escape. Tapping his steering wheel to send a text to Lawson, he suggested a trip to Bud's later. Maybe he'd tell Lawson about Poppy, and maybe he wouldn't, but either way, his eyes would be able to focus on someone other than Poppy Hartman.

What was there to tell Lawson about her, anyway? Poppy was a customer, he was doing a job for her, and he'd finish in a few days, then go home. Maybe they had gone swimming a few times, had lunch, played cards, but the sum total didn't amount to anything worth getting excited about.

He wouldn't mention his experiment to Lawson, but he wouldn't need to. The fact he even mentioned Poppy would give Lawson a heads up since Ham hadn't been interested in any woman for over a year, and Lawson would make encouraging sounds because Ham was taking any kind of interest in a woman, even if he downplayed their interactions.

Lawson's response came soon, saying he'd meet Ham there at seven for dinner. Ham hadn't mentioned dinner, but what the hell. One less meal for him to prepare.

Pulling back into Poppy's driveway, he thought about her offering to make the dump run. Maybe she said it because she was in a hurry to see her floor finished meaning he'd be out of there. Or maybe it was only because she was a nice person. She was a nice person, he knew that, giving him ice water and lunch and making him stop work when the heat index was hellish.

Returning to the porch with the barrels, he knocked, and she was at the door in seconds.

"Hello, again."

"Hey." He watched her walk across the plywood flooring, then squeeze through the furniture stacked in the kitchen before she went out the back door, and he headed into her bedroom to tear out the carpet. He hadn't asked her to remove the bedding, but it would need to be done. She didn't have a heavy headboard and footboard, only a frame, which made it much easier for him, but, as with the couch, he needed to get it out of the way while he worked. Deciding to give her the news now, he headed for the deck, finding her with an unopened book in her lap. "Poppy?"

She turned. "Yes?"

"Can you strip your bed? I need to move it out of the room."

Just the way he'd moved the couch and wooden pieces in the living room. "Right." She left her book outside and followed Ham around the furniture crowded into the kitchen. Growing pains. Making a mess so beauty could be created.

Folding her comforter and sheets, she wondered what she was going to do with them, then decided to stack them on her washer. She should have taken care of this while Ham was gone, but it hadn't occurred to her. "This gets awkward, doesn't it? Having to move everything around when I don't have much space to move it to."

"It'll work out."

Once she'd taken everything she needed, she saw him carry her bed frame into the kitchen, then out onto the deck, and she pictured her bed set up out there, with her sleeping in the great outdoors. If it wasn't for the bugs and possible blowing sand and rain and the complete absence of a sense of security, it might be kind of fun. Maybe for one night.

"This okay out here?"

"Absolutely. You had to do all this with Linc's things, too?"

"Yes."

"How fun for you." Again she'd gotten him to smile. "But then both these jobs must be nonstop fun for you." The way his eyes locked on hers almost made her feel as if she were unable to move.

"No complaints."

When he finally looked away, she felt as if she'd been released from his hold, which was craziness, but she was thankful he returned inside and left her alone with her book. Maybe she'd even open it this time instead of allowing thoughts of Hamilton Wheeler to run rampant in her head.

It amazed Poppy how much Ham had been able to accomplish by six, when he told her he was finished for the day. He'd refused her offer for lunch again, disappearing in his truck for a while, then returning.

Her bedroom floor was finished and the bed was back in position, and half of the living room floor was done, the furniture now out of the kitchen and crowded on the completed half.

The new tile looked so beautiful. Wood-like, but not wood, and it would last for decades while retaining its beauty. She praised his work, possibly excessively, but she loved how it looked and she wanted Ham to know.

Then he backed out of her driveway and pulled into Linc's. She was surprised he'd quit so early, then guessed he must be tired since he'd been working every day for almost two weeks, hard manual labor. Really, the surprise should have been that he took so little time off.

Poppy was having dinner on the deck when she heard a car door slam, and she looked across to see Ham's truck backing out of Linc's driveway. Maybe he was going to get dinner. She stayed on her deck until after the sun had set, a beautiful collection of reds and oranges tonight, then went inside soon after, a little surprised Ham still hadn't returned. No, it was none of her business where he was. But that didn't mean she couldn't speculate about what he was doing.

Ham hadn't had a good steak for a while, and when he took his first bite, he knew the dry spell would continue. Bud's food was adequate, but it wasn't going to win any awards. Still, it was good to be out with Lawson, who'd been filling him in on everything that had been happening at Burnett. The fact Ham hadn't met any of the people Lawson worked with didn't matter, because people were people no matter where they worked, and the stories were always entertaining. And listening gave him time to decide what he wanted to talk about when Lawson finally gave him a chance.

"You dating yet, Ham?" Lawson asked.

Ham was surprised about the abrupt change of subject, and wondered for a half second if Lawson knew something. "No. How about you?"

"Nope." Lawson glanced around. "Any possibilities here? No pressure to do anything about it, but do you see anyone who does it for you? Or is it still too soon?"

After a drink of his Sam Adams, Ham said, "Starting to think it isn't too soon."

Lawson tapped his bottle against Ham's. "Good for you. You met someone?"

"Yes, but it's not going anywhere."

"Why not?"

"I'm doing a job for her," Ham said.

"What kind of job?"

"Working on her house. Minor reno work."

"She married? Is that the problem?" Lawson asked.

"She's single. It's just too soon."

"You realize you just said you thought it isn't too soon to think about dating."

"Feels too soon with her."

"What's she look like?"

Ham suspected Lawson wanted to know if she resembled Veronica, but wouldn't come out and say that. "Dark hair. It's long and it curls up when it gets wet. She's pretty quiet, unless she has something to say."

Lawson grinned. "And how do you know her hair curls when it gets wet?"

"From swimming. She lives next to Linc at the beach."

"And you stand there and watch her?"

"I'm in the water with her," Ham said. "It's a beach. That's how it works."

"I'd like to meet this woman you 'swim' with but won't ask out. What's her name?"

"None of your business." Ham eyed him. Then Lawson laughed, but he laughed alone.

Chapter 24

This was it then. Ham had stretched out the tile job until Friday afternoon, but there was nothing else he could do. The floors looked good, and Poppy repeatedly told him how much she liked them. No, she *loved* them. The weather had turned increasingly warm all week, and even if it hadn't, he probably would have asked Poppy what he was about to ask. "You going for a swim after dinner?" It would be the last time he would swim with her.

"Yes. It's a shame that nice, cool weather is already gone, but it will be good to swim again. Will I see you out there?" Poppy was sitting at the kitchen table writing the check for Ham, and she looked up to meet his eyes.

"I'll be there." When she handed him the check he looked it over quickly, noting she'd added "For a job well done!" in the bottom corner, and he smiled. "Thank you, Poppy."

She stood. "Oh, no. Thank you, Hamilton Wheeler. I will recommend you to all my friends." When she saw his eyes change, she said, "I guess I will *not* recommend you to all my friends. I'll say you're too busy to take on more jobs."

"You could say I've retired because I've reached sixty. Or was it sixty-five?"

"Let's forget about that conversation, shall we?"

Forget it? He was no more likely to forget that conversation than he was every other conversation they'd had. Because there were too damn few of them. "Whatever you say." He folded the check and slid it into his wallet, then gathered his tools and met her eyes again. "See you in the water."

Tonight Poppy would wear her new red tankini, which exposed more of her than her blue one, but so what? She wasn't quite over the hill yet, and she loved the flirty little skirt and the top that only reached her waist, baring a couple of inches of her belly, something she hadn't thought she'd be gutsy enough to wear ever again. When she'd tried it on at the store and looked at herself in the three-sided mirror, Ham's image had popped into her head and she grinned and whispered, "Sold."

Pulling her coordinating towel out of the dryer, she strolled out to the deck, sunglasses in place, and dropped her towel before speed walking over the hot sand to get into the water. She'd beaten Ham out, telling herself that was a good thing since it decreased the self-conscious factor. Holding onto her glasses, she made her dive.

Ham gripped the towel as he stood on the deck, his eyes all over Poppy in a different bathing suit today. The way it swung around her hips and bared her waist deserved his full attention, but too damn soon she was underwater, and he stepped off the deck to go join her. If he wasn't mistaken, there were no straps holding it on, but he needed to be closer to verify that. Who knew when a rogue wave might come in and cause a wardrobe malfunction, and he had to be within reach in case she needed assistance. He surfaced as close to her as he usually did, seeing she was in shallower water tonight, only reaching her waist. "Hey. Nice bathing suit."

"Thanks." Ham had never made such a personal remark and she was a bit flustered. "I don't know if it's my imagination but the water feels colder."

"Maybe from the rain." She was looking over at the same kids they kept seeing, again playing with buckets and shovels, and as he watched Poppy, the look in her eyes changed from amused to the shadowed look he'd seen before.

"I feel like summer's going too fast. But I guess I feel like that every year." Poppy looked at Ham to see he was looking at her. Maybe he agreed. "And you've spent the past two weeks working so hard so you couldn't even enjoy it."

He maneuvered himself closer, wanting to grip her arm or her waist, feel that bare skin. "Is that what you think? That I haven't enjoyed the past two weeks?"

The look in his eyes was so intense it left her momentarily unable to speak. "Have you? Enjoyed them?"

"Yes." He'd enjoyed every second he'd been with her. Every sweet second. Now, the sand was running out of the hourglass and he didn't know what he could do about it since he didn't have the guts to say what he needed to say. "Better than being at Couril. Isn't it?"

"A hundred times better than being at Couril." She wondered if he'd understand that was all because of him. What if she'd hired someone from Home Zone instead of going with Ham's quote? No. She wasn't going to think about that.

Ham thought about asking Poppy to dinner tomorrow, wondering what she'd say. Maybe it really was too soon, as he'd told Lawson. He knew his experiment had been a success, but he still had a way to go to feel ready to ask a woman out. Even one he'd spent as much time with as Poppy.

Poppy guessed Ham had said all he was going to, and they floated silently on the waves, both of them watching the kids as they alternately played well or broke into their little arguments. They were adorable. One little blond boy, and two little girls with light brown hair.

She decided she wouldn't need to have three children. Two would be wonderful. Even one would be wonderful, if that was all she'd have time for before her biological clock ticked its last tock. She and her someday husband would raise that child, or those children, in a home filled with love and patience and trust and joy. But *when*? When was that going to happen?

"You all right, Poppy?" The shadows in her eyes were back again.

"Yes. I'm a little cold. I think I'll go in." She smiled at Ham. "Have a good night."

"Night, Poppy." This was it then. There was no reason to stay in without her, and he swam with her toward shore. Walking beside her until she reached her towel, he wanted to ask her to watch the sun set with him. Or go out for ice cream. Maybe even dinner if he could get the words out. But when she wrapped up in her towel, the one that covered her from neck to knees, then strode through the sand to her deck, he let her go without another word. He picked up his own towel and headed for Linc's deck to dry off. Maybe he'd be lucky enough to catch one more glimpse of her before she went into the cottage and out of his life.

Chapter 25

Poppy woke early on Saturday, another hot one, and planned to be ready for a swim if she saw Ham make any kind of motions toward the water. She hadn't asked him if Linc had any more projects for the next two days, but she could sit out on her deck today, keeping her eyes peeled for any action next door. If and when she saw Ham she could even walk over to say hello.

After showering and dressing, she headed for the kitchen, then went out on her deck for her first breath of fresh air. Casually glancing next door, she didn't see Ham's truck in the driveway, only Linc's Camry, and she guessed Ham had gotten an early start on supplies for whatever he planned to do today.

Cara would be coming over around noon, and Poppy looked forward to sharing parts of what had been going on with Ham because Cara would appreciate the fact Poppy had realized not all men were lying, deceitful losers.

WHEN HAM RETURNED HOME on Friday night, he saw Linc had moved out, probably excited about getting back to his own place. They had either passed each other somewhere between Belvedere and Carmichael, or Linc had gone out with his buddies.

Saturday morning Ham's phone rang while he was having a second cup of coffee on his front porch. "Morning, Linc."

"Ham, thanks for making my place over. It looks fantastic. The guys really liked it, but they wished there were guest rooms so they could stay over."

Ham laughed. "Maybe it's better there aren't any so you don't become party central."

"You're probably right. Anyway, thanks for everything you did. Did you show Poppy?" Linc asked.

"No."

"Maybe I'll ask if she wants to see it. I want to see what you did to hers."

Ham wondered if Poppy would be brought into every conversation he had with Linc. Wasn't it enough that she'd taken up permanent residence in his head? "Do something for me, would you, Linc?"

"Sure."

"Poppy likes to swim after dinner, when everyone else has gone in, and swimming alone isn't safe. Maybe you could keep a subtle eye on her if you're around."

Linc laughed. "Good idea. I'll swim with her, then we'll both be safe."

Ham closed his eyes and leaned back in the rocking chair, wondering how to discourage that idea without Linc catching on.

"See you later, Ham."

Silence on the other end. Ham put down the phone and hoped he hadn't just made a huge mistake.

"POPPY, I LOVE THIS. Your cottage is gorgeous," Cara Norton said when Poppy met her in the driveway. "And it's so good to see you again."

"I'm so happy you could come over. This is a good day to swim and just hang out and enjoy the day."

"I can't wait to see the inside. Your siding is so pretty and new."

Poppy eyed her cottage as they walked to the front door. "The shingles make such a difference and the new wood really refreshes it." Pulling her screen door open, she said, "Welcome to my beach cottage. Won't you come in?"

"Oh, I love it all," Cara said, looking around at the living room and kitchen. "It looks as shiny and bright as a new penny. And look at your view. You must love it here. I certainly would. You've done a beautiful job."

"Thanks, Cara, but I only did the painting. Hamilton Wheeler did the shingles and the floors."

"But you picked out everything, and that's just as important. I love your cabinets, too."

"They're original, but at least they aren't gray anymore," Poppy said.

"And look at the little drawer pulls with the anchors. Those are perfect." Cara reached into her purse and handed Poppy an envelope. "It's a little housewarming gift for you. I hope you can use it."

"Thank you, Cara." Poppy opened the envelope and found a gift card to Home Zone, then gave Cara a hug. "This is *wonderful*. I think I already know what I want to do with this since I need a mirror and an area rug and who knows what else. I love that store. It's like my second home."

"Well, good. Happy shopping."

"What do you want to do first, Cara? Lunch or swim?"

"Let's swim, then eat, then maybe swim again."

"Perfect."

While she and Cara were having lunch on the deck, Poppy glanced over at Linc's driveway for about the dozenth time that day and realized she needed to face facts. Ham must have returned home, since she hadn't seen his truck even once. "So, I mentioned that Hamilton Wheeler did my reno work, which I so appreciate, but what I appreciate even more was the way he helped me in another way." It would have been better if Cara could have seen Ham, but Poppy would still try to make Cara understand even without the visual.

"How's that?" Cara asked, taking a bite of salad.

"You know I was pretty set against men in general after Connor."

"And rightfully so."

"Yes. But Ham, that's his nickname, made me realize there are still good guys out there," Poppy said, gazing at Linc's cottage.

"I am so glad he did that, Poppy, and I'm really happy for you. Did you go out with him?"

"No, no. He was just a really nice guy. And he gave me such a deal on the work he did. He learned the skills working summers in college, but he doesn't do that kind of work professionally. He did buy an old house and gut it, then he did it all over, and he did work on Linc's house next door because Linc is his brother, but his real job is at Couril, which blows my mind."

"No kidding. You didn't recognize him?" Cara said.

"No, I've never even seen him there, but you know how huge that place is."

"Maybe now that you know him, you'll run into him."

Poppy hoped so. She dearly hoped so. "Enough about me. Tell me what you've been doing, Cara. How are things at Burnett?"

HAM HADN'T EVEN BEEN home for twenty-four hours and he was already feeling restless. He went out the back door and took a slow walk around, much like the walk he'd taken with Poppy around her cottage.

Except now Poppy wasn't with him.

He didn't have any upcoming work on her place to look forward to.

His house didn't need any more work done on it.

How the hell was he supposed to fill his time?

Maybe he could build a gazebo in the yard. He had five acres, so there was sure as hell enough space for one. He could build a barn if he really wanted to.

No you can't, genius. You don't have the skills to build a barn.

A gazebo he could manage. But what good was a gazebo if he had no one to use it with?

Would Poppy want a gazebo out back? Probably not, since it would block her cottage's view of the ocean.

Damn.

He needed to come up with something to do before he went stir crazy.

When his phone rang, Ham wondered if he'd be going out to Bud's again. It wasn't his favorite place to be, but it was better than staring at the walls. "Hey, Lawson."

"I don't know if you heard this yet, but Veronica got married today."

Ham stopped walking and stared up at his house, a house Veronica would have lived in with him if she hadn't lied. But she had lied, and he was the only one, other than his family members, who had ever slept there.

It hit him then that the old feelings, the anger, the regret, the bitterness, weren't coming.

They weren't coming.

"Thanks for letting me know."

"You all right about this?"

"Yeah. Yeah, I am all right."

"Good for you, Ham. I need to get back to assembling this freakin' gas grill. Wish me luck."

Ham laughed and disconnected. The experiment with Poppy Hartman had been a rousing success.

And he couldn't even share that with the person responsible.

Chapter 26

Although Poppy wasn't delighted about having to return to Couril on Monday morning after having had two weeks off, she knew working was a fact of life. She also knew how much she would love being in her cottage once she reached home.

The heat wave continued, which meant she'd be taking another swim tonight, one more thing to look forward to. After parking in the Couril garage, she took the elevator and scanned her access card across the pad at the front door, entering the lobby and looking around for possible changes since she'd been there last. No. Everything looked the same.

Taking the staircase to the second floor and the Customer Support office, she wondered if there was any chance she might someday run into Ham. What would she say? Hello and how are you were about all she could say, then she'd feel let down once they separated for their own departments.

What she couldn't say, but what she most wanted to say, was "Why didn't you say goodbye?"

HAM STARED AT THE CHART on his monitor. Hartman, Penelope, extension 46324. Now that he'd located her number, what did he think he was going to do with it? Call and ask if she wanted a gazebo? Maybe a wooden hanging swing? He could use cedar, guaranteeing the thing would last throughout her lifetime.

Maybe she'd end up sharing it with some other guy.

A guy who'd make the shadows in her eyes disappear.

Because a woman like Poppy Hartman was the kind to have and to hold, and he knew she wouldn't remain single for very long.

He closed the company's phone directory and told himself to get to work.

At lunch time, he changed up his route to the front door. He invariably left the building for lunch, and he wondered if Poppy used the company's cafeteria. It could explain why he'd never seen her.

Walking by the caf just after one, he looked in, but since there had to be a couple hundred people either seated or standing in there, spotting one brunette whose hair curled around her beautiful face when it was wet was an impossible task. Pushing his way out the door, he headed for the parking garage, thinking about his experiment.

AFTER DINNER, POPPY pulled on her red tankini and picked up her towel, knowing the water would cool her off as quickly as it always did. As she made her dive into the waves, she wondered when her very last day of swimming would be. Late August? Maybe even early September? She knew September water temps could still be comfortable.

As she floated on her back, Linc's back door opened, then someone was on the deck. Ham?

No. Not Ham. It was Linc. Only Linc. He left his towel on the railing, as he'd done before, then he strode toward her with a wide smile, making a splash when he hit the water.

"Hey, Poppy. How are you?"

"Hi, Linc. I'm doing well, thanks. How are you?"

"Great. Listen, do you think I can take a look at what Ham did to your place sometime? And you can see mine if you want."

"Sure. I'm curious to see how yours turned out."

"I want to see the tile you used."

"You must be happy with yours. I love mine. Ham did a fantastic job."

"Yeah, Ham does great work. Want me to get the beach ball?"

She smiled. "Honestly, I want to just float here and relax. Getting back to work after two weeks off is amazingly challenging."

He laughed. "I hear you. So you want to see my place tomorrow? Maybe around this time?"

"Yes, we can do that."

"Great. I'm going to do some swimming, so I'll see you."

Poppy watched as Linc swam back and forth, parallel to the shoreline, smiling at his energy.

Once she had had enough, she looked around for Linc. Catching his eye, she gave him a wave, which he returned, then she swam to shore. After she'd dried off, she opened the door and looked back to see Linc striding up the beach toward his cottage.

On Tuesday night, Poppy was on her deck after dinner, wondering if Linc still wanted to see her cottage, then she saw him approaching.

"Hey, Poppy."

"Hello."

"Can I see your place? Then you can see mine."

"Of course." Linc followed her inside, and it was interesting to hear his comments and compare them to Cara's. He also noticed the door and drawer pulls, and he squatted to feel the tile, saying he liked the looks of it. He walked around slowly, only peeking his head into the bathroom and bedroom.

"Looks great, Poppy. Are you happy with it?"

"I love it all."

"I wouldn't mind more space, but it works for now," he said. "And it's only my first house. Is this your first?"

She looked away from Linc's gaze. "It's the first I've bought by myself."

"Great choice, right?"

"You're right. It was a great choice."

"Come on next door and you can see what Ham did for me."

Poppy enjoyed Linc's brief tour, making sure he knew she thought it was a beautiful place. The wood floors were gorgeous and polished, and the cabinets looked just like hers. Linc had gone with brushed nickel pulls, and they looked nice and coordinated with the sink. "It's beautiful, Linc. A home to be proud of."

"You're right. And I am proud of it." Heading toward the back door, he said, "I'll walk you home."

"You don't need to, Linc."

"I insist." He pushed the screen door open and walked beside her until they reached her deck. "I was wondering, Poppy. Can I take you to dinner? Maybe this weekend?"

Linc looked so earnest and so young, and she had absolutely not expected anything like this. "Linc, that's very sweet of you, but I'm not ready to date. I do appreciate you asking, though. You have a good night."

"I understand. No problem. Night, Poppy."

She felt his eyes on her until she was inside, then she looked out the window to watch him walk home.

And there went the swimming idea for tonight.

Why did it have to be the wrong brother who asked?

Chapter 27

Ham eyed his phone on Friday after dinner, his head full of thoughts that shouldn't be there, then he called Linc.

"Hey, Ham. What's happening?"

"Just checking in to see how you're doing in your new place." Ham shook his head, wishing he had some imagination.

"Doing great. So you asked me to keep an eye on Poppy when she swims? She only went in Monday night, but I stayed in with her, then when she got out, I got out. Tuesday night I showed her my place and she showed me hers. You did great work on both of them, Ham."

"Thanks." He wasn't sure why he'd called, but it wasn't so he'd be complimented, and now he had images of Poppy with Linc stuck in his head.

"I asked her out but she said she isn't ready to date. Any idea why?"

Ham gritted his teeth. "You asked her out?"

"Yeah, why not? She's hot, she's nice, and she's right next door."

"And she's older than you are, Linc."

"It's not like she's in her fifties. How old do you think she is?"

"I don't know. Older than you."

"Easy there, big brother," Linc said.

"Was Monday the only night she went swimming?"

"Yeah. Do you like her, Ham? Is that why you're acting like this? Maybe you should have said something."

Said something? "It wouldn't matter. As you said, she isn't ready to date."

"Are you ready to date?"

There was a grown up question from his kid brother. "Maybe I am. See you, Linc." After disconnecting, he wondered how ready he was.

Linc asking Poppy out?

Dammit. What if she'd said yes?

She'd never have said yes to Linc. She knew he was a kid.

But it wouldn't always be a kid who asked her out.

Any day now a man was going to come along and ask.

And she was going to say yes.

POPPY NEEDED TO DO something. It was Friday night, it was summer, and she wasn't going to sit at home, even to stare at her beautiful rooms.

She'd go to Home Zone. If she couldn't spend at least an hour there, looking for something to put her new gift card toward, then she wasn't the woman she thought she was. She headed out the door, ready for her adventure.

Grabbing a Home Zone shopping carriage in the parking lot, one of the giant sized ones, Poppy headed inside, deciding the rug section was a good place to start. Parking in the aisle, she had to decide what size and what color she needed. This would occupy her for at least half an hour as she went back and forth because there were too many choices. She wasn't the only one who was feeling home improvement tonight, either. The aisles were full of couples with their carriages.

After sifting through half the selection of rugs, she found it; it had several shades of blue and a lovely cream, a gorgeous Oriental carpet that was the perfect size. She hoisted the heavy plastic wrapped roll and settled it into her carriage, excited about seeing it in her living room.

Since she'd found it so quickly, she'd need to spend extra time in the store, and she headed for another favorite aisle. Adding a mirror or two would make the living room seem bigger, and she could add a few pictures or wall art, maybe with a nautical theme, to complete the look. She could probably spend hundreds of dollars in this store and be delighted with everything she bought. But did she have hundreds of dollars to spend on decorating? She'd have to think about that.

"Poppy?" Ham had never been a believer in wishes, thinking they were for kids, but seeing Poppy Hartman when he'd been spending so much time thinking about her was making a believer out of him.

"*Ham*. Hello. What brings you to Home Zone tonight?" She wondered if he could tell she had adrenaline blasting through her like a ... like a bolt of *lightning* or something.

"Just checking some prices." *Not ready to date.* He needed to remember that. But he wanted to be with her. *Not ready to date, genius*. He gestured to her carriage. "You putting that in your room or the living room?"

"The living room. But you're right. I should get one for my room, too. That tile will be cold in the winter, won't it?"

"Somewhat cold, yes." He wished he could stare at her for the next hour, but he couldn't. She had shopping to do, and only psychos stared at other people and made them uncomfortable. "You need any help getting that in your Jeep?"

"It's not too heavy, but thanks."

He nodded. "Nice seeing you, Poppy."

"It's nice seeing you, Ham. Take care." She watched as he walked away, then forced herself to turn to the side so she'd stop staring at him. *Rugs*. Focus on a rug for the bedroom. It needed to be smaller than the living room rug but still in the blue family. So, back to the rug section. The second one took longer to find than the first, but it was just as pretty in its own way, with a swirly pattern of blue, green, and white. It was gorgeous. Both rugs were gorgeous.

She rolled her carriage to the register, looking around and hoping for another glimpse of Ham, but it didn't happen. Reaching home just as the sun was setting, she hauled everything inside, deciding decorating took precedence over everything else tonight.

Ham had been so distracted by the sight of Poppy Hartman he'd almost forgotten why he'd gone to Home Zone. Remembering he needed another project, possibly a gazebo, lawn swing, or firepit, he realized he couldn't decide which to focus on, and had given it up after walking a few of the aisles.

Then he'd left the store and taken a ride along the beaches in Belvedere. Why not torture himself some more by thinking about the one he wanted but couldn't have?

Chapter 28

Another Friday night, and Ham was again staring at the walls. It had been two weeks since the night he'd seen Poppy at Home Zone, and he knew he couldn't go on like this much longer. Missing her. Wanting her. Needing to be with her.

He could stop in at Linc's and see what his brother was doing, then he could stare at Poppy's house for a while and wonder what she was doing. Or he could just cut to the chase and go see her, ask if she needed help with anything.

Pocketing his keys, he went out the door, wondering if the heat wave was ever going to end. They needed rain, and they needed it soon. His grass was suffering, his trees were suffering, and enough was enough. Starting the truck, he pulled down his long driveway and wished he had control over the adrenaline blasting through him. Rubbing his chest, he told himself to take a few deep breaths and it would ease off.

Sure it would.

Linc's car wasn't in his drive, but the kid was twenty-five and it was Friday night. Poppy's Jeep was in her driveway, though. Alone. Until he pulled in and parked behind it. The sun was about to set, and Ham thought she might be on her deck. Although, just because she used to watch sunsets didn't mean she still did. He walked to her screen door and knocked, wishing the damned adrenaline had slacked off. Then Poppy was at her door, smiling at him, and the adrenaline didn't matter anymore. "Hey."

Astounding. "Hi, Ham. How are you?" Seeing Ham on her porch was absolutely astounding, and she didn't even care that she was probably grinning like a fool.

"Just wanted to check on the shingles. Make sure they haven't fallen off."

"Well, that's such a relief. I was afraid you were here to tell me my check bounced. As you can see, the shingles seem to be holding up pretty well so far."

"That's good."

"Do you want to come in? You could check on the tiles while you're here," she said, watching his face. When he gave her a familiar nod, as he'd done so many times before, she pushed on the screen door. Then he was inside, standing right in front of her. "Can I get you a drink? You're just in time for the sunset."

"Let's see the sunset," he said. "I don't need a drink."

"Come on, then." She heard his footsteps behind her, then they were on the deck, sitting on the Adirondacks. She could tell Ham she still went swimming most nights after dinner, and Linc almost always joined her. She could tell him she stopped swimming for a few nights after Linc had asked her out, then when she resumed because it was silly to just stop, it hadn't even been uncomfortable when Linc joined her. He was a nice guy, seemingly uncomplicated and friendly, and she appreciated having him as her neighbor.

But she wouldn't tell Ham any of those things.

"How's work?" Ham asked, hoping Poppy thought he was watching the sky, and not her profile and the loose curls around her face he still thought about.

"Oh, come on now." She smiled at him. "You know exactly how it is."

"You're right. I do know. We could do much worse than Couril." He wanted to ask where she went for lunch. Who she went with. But he wouldn't.

"It's really beautiful tonight, isn't it?" she asked, making a real effort to keep her eyes forward, not on the man beside her.

"It's a good one." Any sunset with Poppy would be a good one. When the sun disappeared behind the horizon and he continued to sit with her in silence, he wished he knew the magic words to use to get her to agree to go out with him.

"Linc showed me his cottage," she said. "You did another beautiful job in there, Ham."

"I should check on his shingles, too. Maybe the wood floors. Make sure they aren't buckling." Hearing her soft laughter made him smile, despite the gnawing feeling that time was running out for him. After a few more minutes of silence, he stood. "I'll get going. Thanks for sharing your sunset."

Poppy stood with Ham, wishing he'd stay. "Thanks for checking on my shingles. Have a good night, Ham."

"Night, Poppy."

Then he was gone. She heard the truck door slam, then the sound of the engine starting. Pulling her back door open, she went inside, wishing Ham had stayed.

Driving home, he thought about the glimpse of shadows he'd caught in her eyes. He wished he knew what had caused those shadows, and what it would take to make them disappear.

Chapter 29

Another Friday night, and Ham was still alone. And he knew he would remain alone unless he did what he needed to do and said what he needed to say. Heading out the front door, he jumped into his truck and drove to Poppy's house, hoping he found her at home. Alone. And receptive.

He knew Linc had plans tonight since they'd spoken earlier, and he thought if his kid brother could build himself a social life, then he sure as hell should be able to do the same damn thing.

And there was Poppy's cottage ahead, her Jeep in the driveway, with no one else parked in what he'd begun to think of as his spot, and he eased the truck in behind hers.

This time things were going to be different. He was not going to leave disappointed by his failure to say what he needed to say.

This time he rang the bell, hearing it echo through the cottage, then he heard her footsteps approaching. "Hey, Poppy. You have time to talk?"

Ham? Poppy knew she was going to be losing more sleep after this visit, just the way she had a week ago. She put her hand on her chest, feeling the pounding both on the inside and outside. Maybe she was even a little light headed. "Yes. Come in." She stepped back and there he was again, right in front of her, all handsome and quiet and unattainable.

"Were you watching the sunset?" he asked.

"Yes, but—-"

"We can go outside."

"All right." Again, he followed her, but this time he pulled his chair against hers, angling it so he would be able to see her and the sunset.

"Poppy, the last time we sat here together, I saw shadows in your eyes. That wasn't the first time I've seen them, either."

She gave up on the idea of watching the sunset, and stared at Ham. "Shadows?" That sounded bad. She didn't want him to see shadows. She didn't want anything to do with shadows. *Hell's bells.*

"Sorrow. A darkness. Shadows. I see them now." When her shoulders hunched and she folded her arms, he wished he hadn't told her. But he knew if he hoped to get anywhere with this woman, they needed to open up to each other.

Woman up, Poppy. The fact Hamilton Wheeler was with her, wanting to talk and ask questions, was exactly the sign she'd been hoping for, and she would be stupid not to take this opportunity to tell him, no matter how uncomfortable it was going to be. "I was in a relationship for four years. After we'd been together for a year we decided to buy a house and start a family because we both wanted children. Three years later, he told me he didn't want children. He said they would be too much responsibility and we'd lose our freedom to do what we wanted, to go wherever we wanted when we wanted. We had a terrible fight, and we both said some things..." She shook her head. "That was the end. I was devastated, and I couldn't stop thinking I'd lost four years believing I had everything I wanted. Then I was angry with myself for not realizing before then that his words didn't jive with his actions. He never enjoyed seeing kids, watching them in restaurants or just anywhere. After we broke up, we sold the house and I took my half of the money and bought my little beach cottage.

"I still want to fall in love and get married and have children. And I desperately hope I don't fall in love with a man who doesn't want children because I'm not sure I could get past that heartbreak again."

Poppy's story hit Ham hard. He'd suspected she'd had a breakup, but he hadn't expected the rest of it. "Your story is so damned close to my own. My ex and I were planning to get married and have some kids, then I found out I was the only one who wanted them." He nodded at her. "What you went through hurt like hell, Poppy, I know it did. The time we wasted with people who broke our hearts?" He slowly nodded. "I know how much that hurt. But that's in the past now, isn't it?"

Poppy gazed into Ham's eyes. "Yes. It's in the past. But sometimes it still creeps up on me." The shadows Ham had mentioned. Right there in her eyes for all to see.

"Of course it does, Poppy. You were together for four years. We were together for three, and those years don't vanish because we don't want to remember them. But we need to focus on the future. That day I saw your face the first time and you spoke to me, you scared the hell out of me because I wasn't ready to think about another relationship. Then the more time

I spent with you, the more I realized I was ready. And you were what I wanted. I hope like hell there's a chance you might think you and I could be something together. Something special."

Poppy smiled, squeezing his hands. "Yes, Ham. There's an excellent chance we can be something special. I already feel it with you." She was staring into his beautiful eyes, marveling at what was happening, when lightning flashed frighteningly close, brightening the sky. It startled her and she jumped up, tugging Ham with her to the kitchen door, then inside. "Where did that even come from?"

Ham didn't care about the weather. He didn't care about anything but Poppy, and he pulled her against him, his eyes on hers.

One moment she was staring into Ham's eyes and the next his mouth was on hers, his arms pinning her against him. It could have been a rough, fast, hungry kiss, but instead his lips were gentle, tender, and she leaned against him, delighting in the taste and scent and feel of him.

And, oh, those kisses... again and again his lips moved over hers, then he kissed her cheeks and her eyelids and her forehead, then his mouth was on hers again.

Ham knew he wasn't blessed with an excess of patience, but he also knew he wasn't going to rush this with Poppy, because it was too important not to do things properly. What he wanted was to bring her to bed, make love to her, show her how he felt, but he knew that couldn't happen yet. He eased his mouth from hers, looking into her eyes again. "I should go."

"Are you sure?" When Ham smiled, the sweetest smile she'd ever seen, she gave him another kiss, just a quick one. "Is that because you know I'm going to have my wicked way with you if you stay?"

"Yes."

"Well, you're right, and just so you know, it will be happening. Maybe when you least expect it." His smile had lost every bit of sweetness, and now it was teamed with a heavy-lidded look in his eyes. *Hell's bells*. She knew he wanted to go, but she knew he needed to stay, at least for a while. "You did notice it's still storming, right? And you can't go outside until thirty minutes after the last lightning strike. It's not safe."

"How many minutes ago was the last strike?"

"Sadly, I haven't kept track. We can start counting from right now. Meanwhile, we can sit on my couch and think of something to do for the next thirty minutes."

Ham knew what they could do for the next thirty minutes. Hell, for the rest of the night. But none of that was going to happen tonight. He looked at the couch. Denim, comfortable looking, and a length they could get up to some mischief on. A whole lot of mischief. "You still have that deck of cards?" He knew she'd still have it. "We can play War. At the kitchen table." But not until he said what he still needed to say.

She glanced at the couch, disappointed by his plan, even though she knew he was right. That didn't mean she had to like it.

"Poppy, may I take you to dinner tomorrow?"

Finally. "Ham, I would love that. Will we have to play War again?" The grin he sent her was no kind of answer.

Chapter 30

Saturday afternoon Ham sent a text to Linc. "I'm taking Poppy to dinner tonight."

On one hand it felt like a low blow, but on the other, not letting his brother know beforehand felt unkind. He knew Poppy wasn't right for Linc, and not only because of the age difference, and he hoped Linc had realized that.

Linc was quick to send a response. "Nice choice, Bro"

No hard feelings, then. He didn't want to alienate his brother, especially since the two of them lived states away from their parents and sister in Pennsylvania. Linc had decided he wanted to be near Ham and the ocean, and he had relocated to Massachusetts after college, staying with Ham through the farmhouse renovation, then finding his own place. It wasn't lost on Ham that had Linc not found his beach cottage, Ham would not have found Poppy Hartman.

As he was dressing for his date, the phone rang. "Hey, Lawson."

"You up for Bud's tonight?"

"Can't. Got a date."

"Did I get the wrong number?"

Ham would have laughed if he hadn't been so nervous. "Smart ass."

"Ham Wheeler really has a date?"

"I do."

"Good for you, buddy. Who's the lucky lady?"

"The woman I told you about. She lives next door to Linc."

"The one whose hair curls when it's wet?"

"That's the one."

"So you decided it's not too soon to date? That's what you told me before."

"That was a month ago."

"Well, good for you. I hope it works out. You think she has a friend?"

"I can ask. How do you want me to describe you to her?"

"Tell her I'm better looking than you."

Ham laughed. "That won't get you far." He disconnected and finished buttoning his shirt. His fingers slowed as he thought about Poppy's face last night. He'd relived the night multiple times, remembering every detail, including the way the skin around her lips had become irritated and reddened. He knew it hadn't been caused by anything she'd had for dinner, and having done some reading about beards before he'd made the decision to grow his, he had a suspicion he knew what had caused it. He wanted to cover Poppy Hartman with kisses, not beard burn.

He knew why he'd grown the beard, and he also knew the reason was no longer valid. Looking in the mirror, he knew he had a decision to make.

POPPY HAD NEVER BEEN to Rustica, where Ham told her he'd be taking her, so she did a little research and was impressed by the reviews, the menu, and the photos of the restaurant. It looked to be somewhere between fancy and casual, and she wore a red maxi dress with her favorite silver earrings and necklace. Deciding not to give her hair the opportunity to go wild-child on her, she pinned it up in a semi-messy bun.

Then she eased down on the couch, telling herself just because she hadn't gone on a date in over four years, nothing about dating had changed. And she knew Ham well enough not to be nervous. When her doorbell rang exactly on time, she sprang off the couch and opened the door.

Ham was in a navy blue suit looking as if he'd stepped off the page of a magazine. Opening the screen door to him, she stepped back and they gazed at each other, neither speaking for beat after beat after beat, letting their eyes express their thoughts. "I can't call you Ham when you're looking so amazing. You're Hamilton tonight."

"You look beautiful, Poppy. Sultry and sensual. Maybe I need to be concerned about the power of your 'wicked' ways."

Poppy had given a lot of thought about the reason Ham had said he needed to leave last night and she knew neither of them should be too quick to lose themselves in another serious relationship. "We're going to take things slow, because that's the smart thing to do. Then when we do make the decision, I know it will have been worth the wait. But just so you're aware, waiting is going to be excruciating."

Ham took Poppy's hand and pressed a kiss on her fingers. "I'm well aware. Are you ready?"

"To go to Rustica, you mean?" She grinned at him, enjoying the look he shot her. "Yes, Hamilton. I'm really looking forward to dinner with you. It's all right if I call you Hamilton, isn't it?"

Staring at Poppy's face, he wondered why he'd been nervous about their date. "Did you think I'd changed my mind since you asked?"

"Just making sure."

POPPY LOVED BEING ACROSS the table from Hamilton, loved the way he held her eyes, sending her messages she wanted to believe she understood. He was so different than she'd originally thought, even though nothing about his appearance had changed. He had the same thick hair, the same beard, the same beautiful eyes she'd realized at one point were a deep shade of blue. And since the day before, she'd taken special interest in his mouth and the shape of his lips, those lips that had the power to make her lose her mind.

She knew she shouldn't even think about having a long-term relationship with him yet but she couldn't help it. Yes, it was too soon to think about forever, but that didn't stop her from *dreaming* about the two of them being together forever, until death did them part. There was nothing wrong with having dreams. And she could dream about having children with him. Their babies would be adorable and amazing and would make their lives even more complete.

Ham hoped Poppy was enjoying her dinner. His meal was good, or so he thought, but he was more interested in watching Poppy than in what was on his plate. Her eyes drew him in so completely he felt he was losing himself in this woman. Maybe they had only known each other a few weeks, but sometimes that was enough time to know. He wanted a future with her.

He'd had life with Poppy, able to see her and be with her every day, then he'd had life without her, and he didn't need to be a genius to know which he wanted. It also didn't take a genius to realize there was something missing in Poppy's eyes, and he put down his fork and reached across the table, taking her hand. "Poppy?"

"Yes?"

"Last night, I mentioned seeing shadows in your eyes."

As if she'd ever be able to forget a comment like that. "Yes, you did."

"They're not there anymore." He watched her smile widen, and the sight made him wish he could lean across the table and kiss her.

"Because I'm so happy."

"I want you to be happy," he said. "I want to make you happy."

"I am, and you have. You are, Hamilton." She squeezed his hand. "I really wish we didn't have to go slow. But you know what? I'm going to stop whining about it because you don't want to hear me whine. It's not one of my better qualities."

"I'd like to hear more about your qualities."

"I think we should share our qualities. You first, since I told you about whining," Poppy said.

"I can be abrupt."

"All right."

"I was abrupt with you when we met, and I apologize."

"Apology accepted. And I apologize for what I said after you said what you said."

"Apology accepted."

"I can be a little stubborn," she said. "Maybe a lot stubborn."

"Has this been a problem for you?"

Poppy grinned. "Not for me, but other people don't really like it."

"I can be stubborn, too."

"Maybe we can take turns being stubborn," she said.

"We can try that."

"I can be impatient. As you've heard."

"But you can be patient," Ham said. "And you're caring and thoughtful."

"You're kind and caring and thoughtful, and you worked on my house every day until you were exhausted, even on Saturday and Sunday and long into the day and you only charged half of what Home Zone quoted me."

"I wasn't exhausted." Had he looked exhausted?

"Sometimes I talk too much."

"Sometimes I talk too little."

Poppy laughed. This man was wonderful and amazing and she wanted to know everything about him. "We're covering a lot of ground tonight."

"The night isn't over. I'd like to take you out again, Poppy. Tomorrow, and Friday night. Then Saturday afternoon. May I do that?"

"Yes. I'll try not to be stubborn and impatient and talk too much and eat more than my half of dessert."

"What's that? You never mentioned you eat more than your half of dessert."

"Oops."

Chapter 31

On the drive back to Poppy's house, she said, "Thank you for dinner, Hamilton. It was wonderful. Did you have enough dessert?"

"Slicing it down the middle was a smart move. You can't claim you eat more than your half."

"I'm trying to be better for you, Hamilton."

"Don't change, Poppy. Just be yourself, even if it means you'll get more dessert. No pretense, no faking. Just be yourself. Will you do that?" He glanced across the truck at her, noting the pensive look on her face.

"Since you asked so nicely, then I'll always show you the real me."

"Appreciate that," he said.

"At home, can we watch the sun setting, then some TV? That will give us more learning opportunities."

"We'll do that."

Once they were on Poppy's deck, Ham knew he would enjoy watching the sunset more if he had his arm around her. He could pull her into his lap on the Adirondack chair and hold her against him, breathing in the scent of her hair and her skin, but that wouldn't have fallen under the taking-it-slow umbrella. But there was one thing he could do, and he reached for her hand, resting both their hands on the armrest of her blue chair.

Poppy loved holding hands. It was such a simple pleasure that conveyed only positive feelings. Not everyone appreciated the value of that touching, Connor included. Ham's hand was strong and warm and man-sized. Just like Ham himself.

Once the sun had set, she said, "Now we can watch some TV. How about this? You're in charge of the remote and I want you to do exactly what you'd do at home, watching TV alone."

Ham stared at Poppy in the growing darkness, wondering if he was also expected to assign tasks to her. "Let's go."

She appreciated that he hadn't questioned her or argued with her. "I really appreciate it when you open my doors, Hamilton. Do you mind me calling you Hamilton?"

Since she'd asked him a few times, he knew she knew he didn't mind. He wanted to tug on a lock of her hair as his response but the way she was wearing it, all bound up, made that impossible. "Let me think about that and get back to you."

Smiling, she dropped onto the couch, pleased when he slipped off his suit coat and put an arm around her. It was even better than holding hands. Giving him the remote, she anticipated what she might learn about him tonight.

What I'd do at home ... Ham tapped the remote, then went to the guide, scanning through the channels, feeling Poppy's eyes on him. "You aren't looking to see what's on."

"This is about you, Hamilton. As long as you see it, our job will be done."

"This is a job?"

"Maybe job isn't the right word. Maybe it's an experiment."

Poppy using the word experiment had to be a sign that the two of them were on the same track. Seeing the Sox were hosting the Orioles, he made his selection, then put the remote down on the cushion next to him, pulling Poppy a little closer. She felt right tucked against him, and now he could smell a collection of scents from her. He liked every one of them and he thought he could spend hours just sitting like this with her. "How's this? Do you like the Sox? Do you like baseball? Or football?"

"I like watching with someone, but I don't watch by myself."

"Do you want to watch something else?"

You. "This is what I want to watch." Because of the way they were sitting, she couldn't easily watch his face, but she could enjoy the feel of him against her instead. He felt warm and strong and hard and she wished she could put her hands on him, but that would hardly qualify as going slow. *Hell's bells.* When an ad came on, she waited for him to pick up the remote and start checking other channels, but he didn't, and she was delighted. "You don't start clicking away as soon as ads come on?"

"No."

"Why not?"

"Do you?"

"No," she said.

"Why not?"

"You tell me, then I'll tell you."

Ham was realizing Poppy wasn't only interested in the big picture, she needed to know about the small stuff, too. "Sometimes the ads are great, and I don't want to miss whatever I'm watching because I stayed away too long."

"Same for me. I do like some of the ads. What drives me crazy is if I'm watching with someone else and they click through everything after about ten seconds of watching, and then if they find something they want to watch, they still won't sit through the ads. You didn't ask to hear about that, but you might want to know just in case."

"You know what, Poppy? If there's anything else you think I might want to know, just give it to me straight." When she laughed, he cupped the back of her head, pulling her in for a kiss. Just one, and it was a quick one, so his beard wouldn't burn her skin. Leaning back once the game was on again, he guessed he'd made his decision.

After Ham left, with another kiss at her front door, Poppy was a little disappointed they hadn't had a marathon kissing session, but she was pleased to have learned more about him. And she'd shared some of her own little quirks, or whatever they were considered. Habits. Behaviors.

This is me and I hope you like me anyway, kinds of things. There hadn't been a single red flag about the man. And he'd even made her laugh a couple of times.

Oh, Hamilton, you are ringing all my chimes.

And he'd be back at her door the next day at ten to take her on what he'd called a "mystery ride". She couldn't *wait*.

Chapter 32

Never having been on a mystery ride, Poppy had no idea what to expect, which made deciding what to wear another mystery. Settling on a denim skirt and sandals, she packed a small tote bag with jeans and sneakers, then sat on her couch to read until her date arrived.

The man she'd once thought of as a barbarian. Having heard his story, his behavior made sense. Her mother had once told her men were more sensitive than many women realized, and Poppy had been skeptical about those words of wisdom. Until now, when she wondered if maybe her mother had been correct. Hearing the truck in her driveway, she stood, smoothing down her skirt, excited about seeing Hamilton again.

On the drive over, Ham had wondered what Poppy's reaction would be, and if she would even notice. Pressing her doorbell, he heard the chimes, then Poppy was at the door, only inches away from him on the other side of the screen, her mouth open as she stared at him. Yeah. She noticed. "Hey, Poppy. How are you?"

"Color me surprised. Come in here and let me look at you." Although looking wasn't all she was going to do. Seeing Hamilton's smooth shaven face, his angular jawline clearly delineated, his lips on display, she was astounded by how gorgeous he was. She'd thought him handsome with the beard, but she was delighted to be able to gaze at even more of his face and neck now. Tugging on his arm and pulling him inside, she used both hands to stroke his cheeks, her fingertips gliding over the smooth skin. "You look wonderful, Hamilton. Even more wonderful. And you're so smooth. Was your beard too hot for you? I don't know how you've stood it this long, in this summer to end all summers." Pulling her hands back before she made him uncomfortable, she continued to stare at him.

"It was time for a change." He let his eyes travel over her. "You look really nice, Poppy. Really pretty."

"Thank you," she said. "Now I'm going to kiss you, if that's all right. Because I can't help myself." His smile was tender and happy and she stood on her toes and pressed her lips to his. In a heartbeat his hands were on her waist, and one kiss turned into dozens of kisses, until she made the difficult decision to stop before they passed out from lack of oxygen. "So where are we going on this mystery ride?"

"If I tell you it won't be a mystery."

"Then we need to get going, don't we?" In minutes they were in the truck and Poppy watched Hamilton as he backed out onto Surf Drive, then headed away from the downtown Belvedere area. "I like your choice of music, Hamilton. And I'm excited about our ride."

"Good. I am, too." Excited, happy, and hopeful.

What if she hadn't been interested in him and refused to go out with him?

What if she'd started dating Linc instead?

But she hadn't, had she? And she'd made it pretty clear she was very interested. He just needed to make sure he didn't make the mistake of assuming anything, and he needed to make communication a priority. "Poppy?"

"Yes, Hamilton?"

"Thank you for today. Letting me take you out."

When she felt tears prick her eyes she reached over to touch his arm, feel his warm skin, the fine hairs soft under her fingertips. "You're going to make me cry if you say sweet things like that. You should know there's nowhere else I'd rather be than with you."

"Even though you don't know where we're going?"

"Yes. I'm with you, and that's all that matters. Is it too soon to be saying things like that?"

"You can say anything to me," he said. Maybe he could learn a few things from Poppy's excellent communication skills.

"And you can say anything to me."

Despite what she'd said, he knew it was too soon to tell her how he felt, so he'd wait. He wished there wasn't so damn much waiting to get through.

"I hope you don't mind if I stare at you a lot today, Hamilton, but seeing your face after it's been hidden is really, really great. I liked your beard and you looked great with it, but I love seeing your whole face." And feeling his skin against hers.

Ham wondered if he should have just told Poppy where they were headed instead of making it seem as if the day would be something to knock her socks off. "We're going up the coast, and we can stop at Huntley and see their harbor with all the tourist stuff. We can have lunch there, if we see something we like. Maybe get some ice cream. Then stop at a scenic overlook and see the rocky coast. Compare it to what you have in your backyard."

"Very nice. It sounds like so much fun. Maybe they'll have fudge in one of the shops and we can get some."

"We can get anything you want, Poppy."

"I feel like a kid on Christmas morning." His laughter made her laugh, and made her feel all warm and fuzzy.

On their return home, her phone full of selfies and shots of Hamilton she'd be spending a ridiculous amount of time staring at when she was alone, Poppy said, "Today has been wonderful." So wonderful she didn't want it to end. "Would you want to go swimming when we get back? I know a beach that would be perfect."

Hell, yeah. "Swimming would be great. I need to stop by my place to get a couple things." Glancing across the truck at her, he said, "If you're hungry later, maybe we can grab some take-out at the Big Fisherman."

"I already know I'm going to be hungry, so let's do that. Maybe we can watch the sun setting, too."

"We'll do it." When he heard Springsteen's voice, he turned up the volume.

Poppy watched Hamilton mouth the words to "I'm on Fire", one of her favorite Springsteen tunes, and she felt a shiver run up her spine. One day she'd have her chance with Hamilton Wheeler, and she knew they were going to set each other on fire.

But hell's bells, not yet.

Having Hamilton show her his beautiful farmhouse helped to take her mind off her frustration. He'd maintained the character of the exterior and the inside, repurposing many of the old features, and the house was an explosion of charm. She made him show her every gorgeous room and explain every bit of work he'd done, even though she could see he was shy about talking about it. But if he couldn't show off to her, then who could he show off to?

Then they took a walk around his yard, his gigantic yard, and when he said maybe he needed to get some cattle or sheep to keep the grass cut, she'd laughed and that had made him smile. Then he'd kissed her again.

Once he got his things, they headed for her cottage and changed into their suits. When they were playing in the water, Linc joined them for a while before he left to go out with some friends, then Ham said it was time to think about dinner.

After they had dinner on the deck, Ham told Poppy he needed to get going, and she kissed him goodbye at her front door.

It had been a wonderful day, and she hoped there would be more mystery rides.

Chapter 33

Monday morning as Hamilton was shaving, it occurred to him he liked having to do it every day now. After the breakup, when all he'd been able to focus on was putting distance between him and Veronica, hiding behind a beard had seemed like a good plan. He'd begun a new life with a new look, at first not even recognizing himself when he caught his reflection in windows. It was good, the separation between the old and the new.

But now, thanks to Poppy Hartman, he was ready to begin a new life, with another new look. The fact Poppy had seemed to like the change eased his mind, as did the fact the skin on her face had showed no evidence of irritation after last night's round of kissing.

He wouldn't see her until Friday night, which meant five days of waiting. Unless he took a walk to her department at Couril. But to what purpose? Seeing her and being unable to do anything but say hello and ask how she was doing would only be a tease, and he was already dealing with a boatload of teasing. He was crazy about his woman and they'd only been on two dates. *Two dates*. He needed to just dial it back. And maybe if he figured out how the hell to do that, he would.

Poppy wasn't a rebound, he knew that. It had been over a year since the breakup, long enough to get his head on straight and decide how he wanted his life to be. He didn't believe he was Poppy's rebound either, or their initial conversation would have gone very differently. Maybe their first two or three conversations.

He grinned as he remembered their early days and the looks she'd given him. Maybe he'd given her a few looks himself. But he'd come to his senses pretty damn quick, and reminded himself not every woman was deceitful.

Poppy Hartman ...

Damn, he wanted that woman.

But if he stood there any longer daydreaming about her, he was going to be late for work.

AS POPPY STARED AT her monitor on Monday morning, she sorted through a collection of scenarios involving her coming across Hamilton at Couril. All the scenarios followed the same theme. Their eyes would meet in a hallway, or the elevator, or the stairwell, or an otherwise empty conference room. They would jump into each other's arms, their mouths would come together in a kiss that would just about melt the paint off the walls, and they wouldn't be disturbed by any of the thousand other employees for at least, say, an hour.

Their department heads wouldn't wonder why they were away from their posts for so long, and no one would question their disappearances. It would be as if time stood still for everyone but Hamilton and her, and they would make the most of the situation. Even a supply closet would work. If only ...

The more Hamilton kissed her, the more kisses she wanted. But it wasn't only kisses she wanted. It occurred to her there was a talk she and Hamilton hadn't had, and it suddenly became urgent that they have that talk. They had each other's numbers, but so far they hadn't used them, and she wondered if that was unusual for new couples. She wasn't supposed to see Hamilton until Friday night, but she really didn't want to wait that long to ask the burning question. She'd just have to call him tonight, as soon as she reached home. If he said no, then, well, he said no.

But she really wanted him to say yes.

HAM REALIZED AS HE was gazing at the photos of Poppy he'd taken on Sunday that he'd forgotten to ask if she had a friend, per Lawson's request. He wasn't sure how serious Lawson had been, but what kind of friend would he be if he didn't follow through? He wouldn't see her until Friday night, and he knew the question couldn't wait. Wouldn't be fair to Lawson.

He needed to see Poppy tonight so he could ask. He wouldn't have to stay at her place long, just long enough to get an answer. If she was busy, he'd leave. And if she wasn't busy, and she seemed receptive, maybe they'd get dinner.

Having Poppy in his life made him feel seventeen again. Why had he thought waiting until Friday to see her would be a good idea? Seeing her Saturday night then having to wait until Sunday morning at ten had been enough of a hardship. A five day wait was intolerable.

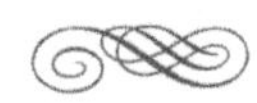

POPPY CHECKED THE TIME on her monitor approximately every three and a half minutes Monday afternoon, and it seemed to take ten hours before five o'clock arrived and she could leave.

Once she was in her car, she took the direct route, for once having no desire to pass every beach in Belvedere to see people at play, and when she finally reached home, she hurried to her bedroom, not sure if she should change her clothes or call Hamilton first. When her doorbell rang, she grimaced at the interruption.

Oh, *my*.

Hamilton was there, and what a beautiful sight he was in his white shirt and navy blue striped tie. Pushing open the door, she pulled him inside, her hand on his bare forearm. "Hamilton, you are exactly the one I wanted to see. I was going to call you, but this is so much better and do you think it's too soon to have the talk about being exclusive because I really want to be exclusive with you."

Damn. It hadn't occurred to Hamilton he and Poppy might be anything but exclusive. "Yes. You and I are exclusive."

If that didn't call for a kiss she didn't know what did, and she cupped his face, feeling just a hint of stubble, then she pressed her mouth to his. Next she felt his arms come around her, and she leaned her full weight against him.

Exclusive.

They were exclusive.

But why had he come over? She released him and looked into his eyes. "I didn't expect to see you tonight, but I'm so happy you're here."

"Forgot to ask you a question the other night."

"What's the question?"

"My buddy, Lawson, asked me to ask you if you had a friend." He realized how absurd that sounded, and he wished he hadn't asked. "You know what? Never mind."

"No, just wait a second. Tell me about your friend."

"Really?"

Poppy smoothed her hand down Hamilton's tie. "Yes. Is he as wonderful as you are?"

Ham laughed. "Depends which of us you ask."

"Does he work at Couril, too?"

"No, he's at Burnett, in Engineering."

"Really?" she asked.

"Yes. Why?"

"My best friend also works at Burnett."

"Is she in Engineering?"

"Accounting." Poppy gazed at Hamilton, wondering what Cara would think about being fixed up. "I'll talk to her tonight and see how she feels about this."

"I'll tell Lawson. What's your friend's name?"

"For now, let's think of her as Mystery Woman."

Ham nodded. "Got it."

"What are your plans for tonight?" she asked.

"No plans. You?"

"If you feel like a burger, do you want to stay for dinner?"

"That would be great, Poppy." But first he needed more kisses.

Chapter 34

"Cara, I have an interesting question for you." Poppy lay on her couch after Hamilton had gone home, feeling as if she were floating. If she could somehow help Cara meet someone who did what Hamilton did for her, well, why shouldn't she try?

"If the question is do I want to meet Hamilton soon, the answer is yes. Your head is so high up in the clouds I need to see what exactly this guy has going for him."

"Everything, Cara. He has everything going for him."

"And that's why I need to meet him, to make sure your head really isn't in the clouds. I'm just looking out for you," Cara said.

"I know, and I appreciate it. And you will meet Hamilton, soon. But my question is, do you know anybody in your Engineering department named Lawson?"

"Not off the top of my head, but Burnett's almost as gigantic as Couril, so it's not unusual."

"Lawson is a friend of Hamilton's, and he asked Hamilton if I had 'a friend', so I told Hamilton I'd see if you were interested in meeting him."

"Really? What do you know about this Lawson?"

"He's in Burnett's Engineering department. That's it."

"Tomorrow I'll do some snooping around and see if I can figure out who he is, then I'll let you know what I find out. Does he know my name?"

"No, I wouldn't tell Hamilton."

"Good girl. This is kind of exciting."

"I think so, too. I hope he's a nice guy and it works out for you," Poppy said.

"Fingers crossed," Cara said.

"YOU COULDN'T GET ME her name?" Lawson asked, and Ham heard the impatience in his friend's tone. He supposed he'd be impatient, too, if he'd had the same dating luck Lawson had.

"No. Poppy will talk to her and let me know what the woman thinks. She's in Accounting there. That's all I got."

"I'll see what I can find out tomorrow. Not even a first name? Hair color? Age? Height?"

Ham laughed. "Not even her GPA."

"Sure. It's funny to you, since you've got yours."

POPPY'S PHONE RANG on the drive home Tuesday and she grinned when she saw the caller ID. "Hello, my friend."

"All right, I'm caving," Cara said. "We have two dozen engineers and I can't go around and ask them all if their name is Lawson and if they have a friend named Hamilton, so I think I'm ready to meet this guy. But I don't want to be alone with him. How about a double date?"

"I'm so happy you're being a brave girl, Cara, and I love the double date idea. I'll talk to Hamilton. What night would be good? You want dinner, right? Then if it doesn't work out, you can escape after an hour or so."

"Dinner is good and I can do any night this week," Cara said.

"I'll let you know." Once Poppy reached home, she picked up her phone to call Hamilton for the very first time.

"Poppy. Great to hear from you."

"Hi, Hamilton. How was your day?"

"Typical. How was yours?" he asked.

"It was good. I just talked to Cara, and we thought a double date would be a good way for Cara and Lawson to meet."

Cara. Now Ham had a name for Lawson. "I'll call him. When do you want to do this?"

"Tomorrow? Thursday? Whatever works. Cara can do either night."

"I'll call you once I have something."

"Have a good night, Hamilton."

"Night, Poppy. Sweet dreams."

"HOW ABOUT DINNER TOMORROW night? And her name is Cara," Ham said as soon as Lawson answered his call.

"Cara, huh? Tomorrow works. Where am I taking Cara?"

Ham hadn't discussed that with Poppy. His first thought was Rustica, but he thought of that as Poppy's and his place. Big Fisherman might work, but what if Cara had seafood allergies? "I'll text you. And it'll be the four of us." After he disconnected, he called Poppy.

"Hi, Hamilton."

"Hey, Poppy. Dinner tomorrow is a go. Where are we going?"

"How about Big Fisherman?"

"That works," he said.

"I'm going to drive with Cara and meet you there, if that's all right."

Ham guessed it would have to be. "How's six o'clock?"

"That sounds great. I can't wait to see you again."

Maybe she wouldn't have to wait. He could ask her out for dinner right now. He was about to suggest the idea when he heard Poppy's doorbell ring in the background.

"My parents are here."

"I'll see you tomorrow. Sweet dreams, Poppy."

"Good night."

Ham walked into the kitchen, disappointed he'd be eating alone. It occurred to him he hadn't had to make dinner since Friday, so he guessed it was time. First he texted Lawson. "Big Fisherman at six."

After he received a thumbs up, he put the phone away and stared at his dinner options. Nothing looked good. He told himself to snap out of it and make himself some damn dinner.

Chapter 35

Poppy should have realized the double date wasn't going to provide enough of a Hamilton fix as she wanted, but Wednesday night wasn't about her, it was about Cara and Lawson. Although every time Poppy looked at Hamilton she found him looking at her, and the look in his eyes made her feel as if they were the only ones at the table.

Cara smiled a lot, and Lawson seemed to keep his eyes on her during the meal, only addressing a few remarks to Hamilton, and almost none to Poppy. Poppy looked forward to hearing what Cara thought of Lawson on the ride home.

After Hamilton walked Poppy to her Jeep, he tilted her chin up and gave her a kiss. "Sweet dreams, Poppy."

"Good night, Hamilton."

Then she and Cara were in the Jeep and on the way home. "So? What did you think?" Poppy glanced at Cara, who was leaning her head back, smiling.

"Thank you for setting me up with Lawson."

"I don't detect any sarcasm."

"There is zero sarcasm. I like him, Poppy."

"That's great."

"He told me he'd call me," Cara said.

"He got your number?"

"He asked me for it on the way to the car. And if he calls and asks me out, I'll go."

"Good. He looked like he couldn't take his eyes off you, and I hoped you were having fun."

"I was having fun and he is one nice looking guy. How about you? Did you have fun? Hamilton seems great, and he was staring at you like crazy. Clearly he's head over heels for you, just the way you are for him. But what about his famous beard?"

"He just shaved it off over the weekend. I'm still getting used to his new look."

"Was he giving you beard burn when he kissed you? Is that why he shaved it off?" Cara asked.

Beard burn? She thought about the first time they'd kissed and the redness she'd seen on her chin afterwards. Had Hamilton noticed? That couldn't have been why he'd shaved, could it?

"When are you and Hamilton going out next?"

Poppy refocused on the conversation. "Friday night." She made a right turn onto Cara's street.

"Well, I hope you have a wonderful time."

"Thanks, Cara." She parked the Jeep by the steps of Cara's apartment building. "Let me know if you hear from Lawson. Bye."

"You'll be the first to hear. Night, night."

Once she was home, Poppy really wanted to talk to Hamilton, but she didn't want to bother him if he was still with Lawson.

When her phone rang while she was brushing her teeth, she was happy to see his number. "Hello there."

"Hey, Poppy. It was a good time tonight."

"I had fun, and Cara did, too."

"Lawson's going to ask Cara out. He said he likes her."

"Good. She'll say yes."

"Tomorrow, can we have dinner again? Takeout?"

"I'd love that, Hamilton. Tonight was fun, but it wasn't just *us*."

"Tomorrow will be just us," he said. "Maybe we'll catch the sunset. We missed it tonight."

"I know, and I feel like the Earth is tilted the wrong way."

"I didn't get to kiss you, either. Not enough, anyway."

"Tomorrow night we'll watch the sun set and we'll do lots of kissing," she said.

"Promise?"

"I promise."

As soon as she disconnected, she had a call from Cara.

"Hello, my friend." Poppy smiled, knowing what Cara was going to say.

"Lawson called and we're going to dinner Friday. I'm pretty excited about it."

"That is exciting, Cara. I hope you have a wonderful time." When she heard Cara's loud, happy sigh, she laughed. "Yes, I know. It's all magical, isn't it?"

Chapter 36

They ate Thursday night's dinner on the deck, their chairs pushed together, but Poppy still wanted to be closer to Hamilton. There were a few people out on the neighboring beaches, but the evening was pretty quiet, and she wondered if summer was winding down already. She and Hamilton didn't speak as they ate, both of them watching the waves, and she could picture herself sitting on her deck in the fall, still watching the waves, maybe wrapped in a blanket. She hoped Hamilton would be right beside her.

After dinner had been cleared away, they returned to the deck, and Ham took the white chair, watching Poppy in her chair for a couple moments. "Poppy?"

"Yes, Hamilton?"

"This would be a lot better if you were in my lap."

"You don't think I'll crush you?" He was silent for so long she wondered if he was going to answer. Then he looked away from her, smiling.

"Do I have to come over and get you?"

"I'd like to see you try," she said.

Ham bent to pick up Poppy, then she laughed and jumped up into his arms. After he'd sat again she settled in his lap and he closed his eyes, loving the feel of her against him. This was both the best and the worst idea he'd had recently. "You comfortable?"

"Am I squashing you?"

He felt the tension in her muscles and wondered what she thought she was going to do next. "Relax. Let me just..." He shifted himself and her slightly. "That better?" It sure as hell was better for him.

Oh, yeah ...

Exquisite torture, every sweet second.

Poppy relaxed against Hamilton, resting her head on his shoulder, enjoying the feel of his chest against her back. Then she felt his hands slide around her until they were spread against her belly. Oh, that was even better. And when he turned her head so his mouth could cover hers, she forgot all about watching the sun set.

POPPY KNEW THERE WOULD be no deck time on Friday night, no sunset viewing, no sitting in Hamilton's lap, since it had been pouring all day and was supposed to continue throughout the night. As she sat at her desk, she thought about her backup plan; her couch. It would do very nicely.

What was a real shame was they wouldn't be moving to her bedroom. Being with Hamilton and having that stupid we-need-to-go-slow plan was making her lose her mind. The way he looked, the way he smelled, the way his eyes were all over her, saying exactly what she wanted him to say, were all combining to make her wonder how she was going to get through this.

They hadn't discussed when this going slow process would be coming to an end, and she wondered if she should bring that up tonight. Maybe if she had an end date, a light at the end of this tunnel of lust, she'd be able to pace herself and make it through.

When her desk phone rang it startled her, and she came out of her head and got back to work.

AS HAM DROVE TO POPPY'S house for their Friday night date, he thought about their plan to take things slow, and as he did every time he thought about the damn plan, he wondered just how vital it was. Did he really believe making love to Poppy was going to ruin their relationship?

Hell, no. It could only deepen it.

When he pulled into her driveway, he saw her standing at the screen door, and he ran through the rain to get to her. "Hey, Poppy." He pulled her into his arms before she could speak, then he kissed her the way he'd been wanting to all damn day.

Once Hamilton released her, she put her hands on his chest as she caught her breath. "Happy Friday, Hamilton."

"You, too. It's damn good to see you."

"I know you wanted to go to the Scupper, but do you think we can stay in tonight and get a delivery? Then watch some TV?" Or maybe skip the TV part and make out like teenagers.

"We'll stay in." Ham pulled out his phone. "What do you feel like?"

You. But he wasn't on the menu yet.

Once Ham made the call, both of them still standing by the door, he glanced at the couch, knowing he and Poppy would be spending some quality time there tonight. "Want to sit?" No sense wasting time.

Poppy tugged Hamilton to the couch and they were in each other's arms in an instant, then he stretched them both out and pulled her closer. "This is perfect, Hamilton."

He didn't release her mouth until the doorbell rang with the delivery.

"I'll get the door." Ham maneuvered himself off the couch and brushed a hand through his hair. "Thanks." Taking the bag from the kid, he closed the door and looked at Poppy, still stretched out on the couch. He wanted to forget dinner and carry her to the bedroom to finish what they'd started about twenty times already. "Hungry?"

She knew Hamilton had to be hungry, and she supposed she was hungry, too. "Yes. Kitchen or couch?"

"Kitchen. Then couch."

The smile he gave her went right to her bones and she wondered if her knees were strong enough to get her off the couch. But Hamilton was there, reaching for her, and he wrapped his free arm around her for the few steps to the kitchen.

After dinner Poppy reached the couch first, and she patted the cushion next to her, as if Hamilton was going to sit anywhere else. "I need to ask you something."

"What is it, Poppy?"

"It's about the first time you *really* kissed me."

"I remember it well."

She was relieved when he smiled. "I noticed that night after you left my chin was kind of red, and since I've never kissed a man with a beard before, I wondered ... Anyway, I wondered why you shaved your beard. You would have had to see the redness, and I wondered if that was why you shaved." When Hamilton took her hand, she looked from their hands to his eyes.

"There were a couple reasons, and that was one of them. I have plans for you and giving you a rash wasn't part of the plans."

He'd shaved his gorgeous beard for her? Even if he had another reason, he'd still done it for her. "Hamilton, I love you."

Poppy's words went right to his soul, and he gripped her shoulders. "I love you, Poppy." Pulling her down on the couch, he covered her mouth with his, tasting her sweet lips, his tongue tangling with hers. He wanted her, all of her, but he knew he couldn't have her. Not yet. But soon. Dammit, it had to be soon.

She loved him and he loved her and she was feeling bold. Rolling on top of Hamilton, she pressed her full length against him. Oh, this felt even better.

Until Hamilton lifted her seconds later and slid out from under her, then he was standing beside the couch.

This was killing him. "I have to leave, Poppy. I'll see you tomorrow at two." Bending to press one quick kiss, and only one kiss, on Poppy's mouth, he headed for the front door, closing it quietly behind him. He could stand in the rain for a few minutes, or he could go home and take a cold shower.

The decision was easy.

Hell's bells and wishing wells.

Poppy stared at her front door and reviewed what had just happened. She needed to make up her mind about a couple of things.

The decision was easy.

Chapter 37

As he drove to Poppy's house on Saturday, he wondered if he should end all his dates with her by jumping in the ocean, fully clothed. Driving home soaking wet, dripping all over the leather seats of his truck, might help him focus on something besides his mounting frustration. He wondered how Poppy was dealing with her own frustration. He knew she felt it. He could see it in her eyes, feel it in her touch, hear it in the little sounds she made, all of which served to make him lose his mind.

Maybe he needed...

Hell, he knew what he needed.

He knew exactly what he needed.

POPPY WAS WATCHING out the window, and she spotted Hamilton's truck coming when he was about four houses away. She'd gone shopping earlier, too early for the store to be open in fact, and had stood outside the locked door, waiting for the store employees to unlock it, then she charged in, headed for the lingerie section. As soon as she spotted it, she knew it was exactly what she needed.

Stepping toward her front door, aware Hamilton's truck was in her driveway, she gave her outfit one more check. Actually, it couldn't be considered an outfit. She wasn't sure what it was, other than a bit of sheer white lace with sleeves that showed everything she had. She hadn't bothered with panties or a bra, because there was no point.

And she was going to make her point, and Hamilton was not leaving her the way he'd left her last night. She understood why he had left, and on one hand greatly admired his strength of character. On the other hand, she'd had about enough of his strength of character.

She had lit a vanilla candle, she was in her battle gear, and she was ready. When the doorbell rang, she whipped open the door and watched Hamilton through the screen, hoping she saw what she hoped to see on his face.

Ham was pretty sure he'd lost the ability to move. Except for his eyes. His eyes were all over Poppy in whatever the hell she barely had on. It was white, he could see that, and he could see every inch of her beautiful skin since she was naked under it.

She was the most beautiful woman he'd ever seen.

Dammit, he needed another cold shower.

"Hamilton, life is short. I am thirty-five years old, I know what I want, and I want you. No more going slow. I need you to come in here and take me." She reached to open the screen door but Hamilton was quicker.

Once he was inside, he slammed her front door and scooped her up into his arms, just the way she'd always wanted to be picked up, loving the firmness of his chest and arms, then he carried her to her room and set her down next to her bed. His eyes, then his hands, slowly slid all over her, then he met her eyes.

"I love you, Poppy. You're so beautiful." Ham pulled off his polo shirt and dropped it on the floor, then Poppy reached for the button on his shorts.

"I love you, too, Hamilton."

Then his mouth and his hands were on her and he whispered sweet words in her ear as he eased her onto the bed, just the way she'd imagined.

HAMILTON FELT POPPY stir in his arms. Maybe she was awake, and he moved his head back on the pillow far enough to be able to see her face. That face. "Hey."

Poppy met Hamilton's eyes. What gorgeous eyes. What a gorgeous body. "Hi there, handsome. You know, you were pretty impressive before with your shingling and tiling, but what you've done here today has really exceeded my expectations."

"I'm not done yet, sweetheart." He slid his hands to her waist, loving the feel of her skin.

"I'm happy to hear that. We still have plenty of time until the sun sets. In case you wanted to catch the sunset tonight."

"We can discuss it later."

"Did you have plans for today?" she asked. "I know I had plans of my own, but you might have had some plans, too."

"My plans were along the lines of your plans. Now that we've done your plans, it's time for mine."

Poppy realized with the first touch of his lips she was one hundred percent in favor of Hamilton's plans.

Chapter 38

Ham stood in the kitchen and tapped his phone, then waited for Lawson to answer. He had no idea if Lawson was with Cara tonight, but he supposed if his friend didn't want to be disturbed the call would go to voicemail. Except this wasn't something Ham was going to leave a message about.

"Ham. What's going on?"

"Couple things. Are you alone?"

"Cara's with Poppy tonight. What do you need?"

Right. Ham knew that, and if his head had been on straight he wouldn't have forgotten. He liked the fact Lawson assumed he was asking if Lawson was with Cara. It made him feel better about what he was about to ask. "Just an opinion. You've got plenty of them to go around."

"Too true, brother."

"You've been going out with Cara for what now? A month or two?"

"Try four months," Lawson said.

Which only reinforced Ham's idea he was doing the right thing. "Poppy and I have a month on you."

"Is this a contest?"

"No. Just thinking aloud." He looked at his reflection in the kitchen window. "Poppy's the one, Lawson."

"That's great news, buddy. Whenever I see you two together, she looks like she's got stars in her eyes. Who the hell knows why."

Ham laughed. "Yeah. I want to ask her to marry me."

"What do you need from me? Kinda busy with my own girl, here."

Lawson was a real riot tonight. "I don't know if it's too soon to ask."

"You love her? Stupid question, since she's all you talk about," Lawson said.

"Yes, I love Poppy. Course I do. And I want to spend the rest of my life with her. She wants kids, just like I do. She's everything I want."

"So give me three reasons why you'd want to wait to ask her."

Three reasons why I would wait to ask?

"You still there, Ham? I'm not hearing anything."

"Nothing. I've got nothing." He smiled. "I guess I have my answer."

"I guess you do. Did you get a ring?"

"That's next."

"Good luck."

"I don't need luck. I just need Poppy." And maybe to figure out what kind of ring to get her.

Ham spent some time researching the engagement ring process, feeling more confident because he now had what he thought he needed. Once he finished, he double-checked the time, seeing it was after midnight.

Tomorrow after work he'd head to the jewelers and see what he could find.

Except he had a better idea, and he logged back on to Couril's website to put in for personal time. Then he went to bed, hoping he wasn't awake the rest of the night thinking about Poppy's answer.

Heading into Boston, after having approximately four hours of sleep, Ham hoped he didn't need an appointment or his lack of patience was going to be on display.

Two hours after walking into the building, Ham walked out with a tiny box in the pocket of his jacket and the assurance if Poppy didn't love the ring, they could bring it back. He shivered as he walked back to the parking garage, wishing he'd worn a warmer coat.

He wondered when Poppy would want to get married. Early June, when they met? Early December, twelve months from now? Maybe somewhere in between?

Should he have given her father a heads up? Probably not. Seemed like an old fashioned thing to do. He and Poppy had had dinner with her parents a few times, and he liked her mom and dad. He thought they liked him.

He'd brought Poppy home to Pennsylvania to meet his parents, and he knew his parents liked her. Since everyone liked everyone else, it seemed as if things were happening the way they were supposed to.

But he needed to wait until the weekend so they'd have plenty of time and opportunity to do what they had to do.

Married.

He was going to be married to the woman of his dreams.

Life was pretty damned wonderful.

Reaching home, he saw he had a few hours until Poppy was home from work. They didn't have plans, but maybe she'd want to get dinner with him. Since the Big Fisherman had closed in early November, that was out. But she liked the Scupper, especially the big Christmas tree the place had in the dining room because it was on a rotating tree stand, and Poppy had told him she could watch it turning for hours, so maybe that would work. Tapping his phone, he sent her a text. "Dinner at the Scupper?"

While he waited for her response, he opened the tiny box again and stared at the ring inside, hoping she liked it.

Hoping she said yes.

Hoping they could be married before he had another birthday, although maybe that was asking for too much. As long as Poppy said yes, he'd wait out the time until they were married and living in the same house. One more thing they'd need to figure out.

When his phone vibrated, he saw Poppy's response. "Yes! 6?"

"See you then. I love you."

"I love you, Hamilton."

That was settled. Now he just had to wait until a quarter to six so he could get in the truck and go get his woman.

Chapter 39

"How was work today?" Poppy asked Hamilton across the wooden table at the Scupper.

Ham knew he had a poker face. He'd been accused of being emotionless by more than one girl, but facing Poppy now after a question he hadn't expected to be asked might well be what gave him away. "Did I tell you how beautiful you look tonight?"

"You may have mentioned that. Did I tell you how handsome you look tonight? There's an extra sparkle in your eyes."

Damn. Would she be able to guess what was going to happen after dinner? "Must be the company I keep."

Poppy laughed, then looked at the menu. "What did you decide to have tonight?"

I thought I'd have a fiancée. But not until we get home. "Going with the ribeye. What are you having?"

I'll be having a big, strong man in my bed in about an hour and a half, if all goes well. "Maybe the chicken pot pie. It's a good cold weather food and it might help me feel less sad because we have to wait five months until May is here again. Not that we can swim in May, but we can be outside and watch the sunsets again. Maybe even in April, if we have a really nice day."

"You like your sunsets, don't you?"

"I especially like them with you," Poppy said.

If he were a patient man, he could wait until Saturday, when the sun would set at around 4:30, and he could ask Poppy the all-important question on the deck.

That was never going to happen.

It was going to be tonight.

In Poppy's living room.

As they ate their meals, Poppy wondered if Hamilton's mind was somewhere else tonight. He hadn't answered a couple of her questions, but he'd worn a sweet little smile for much of the meal, something different. She'd be patient and not pester him about it, just enjoy the smile and the way his eyes were almost glittering. "Hamilton?"

"Yes?" Ham lay his fork and knife on his now empty plate, wondering how his dinner had disappeared so quickly.

"Friday, can we start another vacation weekend at your house? I want to look at your Christmas tree with the fireplace going." Poppy had realized with the cold on-shore winds of late fall, her little cottage wasn't all that toasty warm, and she feared only insulation and new windows were going to solve that issue. Neither of which she was prepared to invest in now.

"We'll do it. We can stay in all weekend if you want." Poppy's so-called vacation weekend requests were becoming more frequent, and they usually entailed cooking meals together in between extended stays in his bed. He'd asked her a few times if she wanted to move in with him during the cold months, and even beyond, but she'd been reluctant so far.

"Yes. All weekend, once we do our grocery shopping on Friday night."

As Hamilton drove them home from the restaurant, she thought about how much she adored staying over at his farmhouse, and she couldn't wait for the weekend to come. Making meals with him, sitting in front of the fire, with or without the TV on, then being in his bed together, was all wonderful. He was wonderful.

Walking from his truck into her cottage, she shivered when a gust of wind hit her. "It's so freezing tonight. I can't wait to snuggle with you so I can make sure to keep you warm."

Ham knew he should laugh at her comment, and if he weren't so wired about what was about to happen, it would have happened naturally. But he didn't think he was capable of faking a laugh. "Just thinking about it is warming me up."

Once they were inside, Poppy hung their coats in the closet, then they sat on the couch and she covered their legs with the plush blanket that had become a fixture on the back of the couch. "There. That's better. Do you want some tea or hot cocoa to warm you up?"

"No."

Hamilton's answer was so uncharacteristically abrupt that she turned to face him. "Is anything bothering you tonight, Hamilton? You don't seem yourself. Is there anything I can help you with?"

Ham gazed into Poppy's eyes, but his mind wasn't on whatever she'd just said.

One knee.

Ask her.

Offer ring.

Now.

He slid off the couch and pulled out the tiny box, the velvet soft in his palm. Then he was in position and Poppy's eyes were wide open. *Good.*

"Poppy, I love you very much. You are beautiful, kind, caring, smart, funny, and I want to spend the rest of my life making you as happy as you make me. Will you marry me?" Keeping his eyes on her face, Ham opened the box and held his breath.

Oh, my heart ...

Poppy had hoped one day Hamilton would propose, of course she had, because she loved him with all her heart and had dreamed about being with him forever. "Yes, Hamilton. I love you like crazy and I would love to marry you, you gorgeous, wonderful man. Yes, yes, *yes.*" She leaned forward and pressed her mouth to his. "Yes. Yes, *please.*" When she felt his fingers on hers, she looked down and saw him sliding a stunning diamond solitaire on her finger. "Oh, look at it. It's perfect. I love you, Hamilton."

Ham joined Poppy on the couch, taking her in his arms. "I love you, too, Poppy. We're going to see a hell of a lot of sunsets together, aren't we?"

"Yes, we are, sweetheart." Then Hamilton's mouth covered hers and he scooped her up and carried her to her room. Just as she'd imagined he would.

Don't miss out!

Visit the website below and you can sign up to receive emails whenever Diane M. Pratt publishes a new book. There's no charge and no obligation.

https://books2read.com/r/B-A-IDWJ-AGUMC

BOOKS 2 READ

Connecting independent readers to independent writers.

Also by Diane M. Pratt

Another First Impression Out the Window
Kiss Me Lots
Beach Rights Included
Prelude to a Courtship
Miss Understandings
It Began with a Man in a Tent
It Began with a Man in a Snowbank
It Began with a Man in a Photo
It Began with a Man in a Loft
It Began with a Man in a Wedding
It Began with a Man in a Lemonade Stand
It Began with a Man in an Attic
It Began with a Man in a Backyard
Sundance Island
Just a Glance Away
Comedy of Errors
It Began with a Man in a Beach Town
It Began with a Man in a Mansion
Unfinished Business
It Began with a Man in a Contest
It Began with a Man in an Office
It Began with a Man in a Pickup
It Began with a Man in a Mall

It Began with a Man in a Village
It Began with a Man in a Cabin
It Began with a Man in a Raffle
It Began with a Man in a Barn
Losing the Freshman Fifteen
It Began with a Man at a Lake
It Began with a Man on an Island
It Began with a Man in a Suit
Kissing Frogs and Princes
It Began with a Man and a Sax
It Began with a Man at a Bonfire
It Began with a Man in a Bookstore
It Began with a Man at a Festival
Romance is Afoot
It Began with a Man Next Door
Once Upon a Text
Once Upon a Competition
Once Upon a Road Trip
Once Upon a Masquerade Ball
Once Upon a Trip to Vegas
It Began with a Man in a Townhouse
Once Upon a Beach

About the Author

Diane M. Pratt lives on Cape Cod where she avoids the summer traffic by hiding at home with her trusty laptop, long-suffering husband, and all the chocolate she can find. Escaping from reality in a romance novel, the ultimate goal a happy ending, is her idea of a good read.

Milton Keynes UK
Ingram Content Group UK Ltd.
UKHW011940240823
427419UK00001B/17

9 798223 057659